THE BIG GOODBYE

When gorgeous Juanita Morales arrived in Monkton City looking for bright lights and glamour, she found herself mixed up in an elaborate racket and finally murder ... Mark Preston didn't mind so long as women like Dixie Whitton and Sylvia Le Fay kept cropping up. He minded more when a fat man stuck a pistol in his face, and ice-picks in the back became the things to wear. Preston was on thin ice, because Rourke of Homicide was muttering about jail ... And of course there were still more dames.

PETER CHAMBERS

THE BIG GOODBYE

Complete and Unabridged

LINFORD
Leicester

First published in Great Britain

First Linford Edition
published 2006

British Library CIP Data

Chambers, Peter, *1924*–
    The big goodbye.—Large print ed.—
Linford mystery library
1. Detective and mystery stories
2. Large type books
I. Title
823.9′14 [F]

ISBN 1–84617–188–1

Published by
F. A. Thorpe (Publishing)
Anstey, Leicestershire

Set by Words & Graphics Ltd.
Anstey, Leicestershire
Printed and bound in Great Britain by
T. J. International Ltd., Padstow, Cornwall

This book is printed on acid-free paper

Prologue

The party was in full swing. A svelte blonde and a middle-aged man in a white tuxedo were giving an energetic demonstration of the Charleston. Canned music blared above the raucous encouragement of the other revellers. As an exhibition of dancing it might have fallen a little below professional requirements, but the blonde was giving it everything she'd got, and the men present were not going to be too exacting about the steps while they could gorge their eyes on the plentiful display of her natural charms. Her partner puffed willingly along, a fatuous grin on his heavy face as he jerked and cavorted more or less in time with the music.

'C'mon Blondie, perk it up.'

'Keep going Ches, you're catching her.'

'Man, look at that blonde go.'

The room was a blaze of light. All around the dancing pair, men and women stood cheering them on. Some were beating out the tempo with their hands, others were locked in each others arms, swaying slightly with the music. A bar had been erected in one corner, and here stood a white-jacketed waiter, smiling and putting his bottles in order. He knew that once the dance was over everybody would be clamouring for a refill. To these people it might be a once-yearly big night out, but to him it was the usual evening chore.

'Ten bucks it'll happen if she leans over any further.'

'You got a bet. Go, girl, go.'

Slightly to one side a small group of four men stood, drinks in hand, watching the scene. In white evening jackets, like most of the men, these were somehow apart. For one thing they were the only ones without women and there was no evident reason why that should be. Even the oldest man seemed to have a girl with him, and these four were by no means old. They seemed detached. Everybody else was in the party, of the party. The four were merely at it. And of the four, one was the leader. The others acted as a background to him. Even a casual observer would see that at once. The man on his right turned slightly towards him.

'You think it's O.K. in there?'

He nodded towards a closed door at the far end of the room away from the revellers. The leader of the group, some years younger than the man who'd addressed him, stared at the other coolly.

'What exactly do you mean, is it O.K.?'

'Well, you know, we've never had any trouble — '

'Exactly. We've never had any trouble, and we're not going to have any tonight. Even if something goes wrong, it won't mean trouble. Not for us, remember that.'

'Sure, yes, I guess you're right.'

The questioner resumed his study of the dancers. The girl was working up to her full pitch now, and several of the men had ceased the handclapping. They were staring at the long slim legs and bouncing full breasts with slightly glazed expressions. The change did not go unnoticed by the leader. He spoke to the man on his left.

'The blonde is O.K. What's her name?'

'Sylvia, boss. Sylvia Le Fay.'

'When she's through with the chump, I want to see her.'

'Shall be, boss.'

Even as he spoke the henchman saw from the corner of his eye a movement as the far door opened slightly.

'Boss.'

In response to the whispered word the leader half-turned his head and saw a man peering out at the party.

'Go take a look.'

The man on his left walked away. His movements were casual but smooth. Within seconds he was back. Some of the forced good humour had evaporated.

'You better come, boss,' he spoke in a low voice. Then as the others moved to join their leader he added, 'Just you, boss.'

The boss caught something in his tone and nodded quickly.

'All right. You boys wait here. I'll give you the buzz. Keep this mess brewing out here. Tell the blonde to take it all off if she has to, but I don't want anybody poking their snoots in there. You got it?'

'Got it,' chorused the two.

4

He strode towards the half-open door. The henchman, a much shorter man, had to scuttle to keep up with him. The two of them went inside and sealed away the noise of the party. Inside, a stout middle-aged man was slumped in a high back chair. His head was buried in his hands and his body trembled violently. He didn't even bother to look up to see who was keeping him company.

'What happened, Mr. Compton?' enquired the leader sharply.

The stout man shook his head violently and a sob escaped from between the clenched hands. The boss nodded towards the shaking figure, and Shorty went across and grabbed him by the shoulder. Not too gently. Surprised at the sudden physical contact, the man in the chair pulled himself together sufficiently to attempt an upright position. Boss stood in front of him.

'Like to know what happened, Mr. Compton,' he repeated. 'You ready to talk now?'

Compton opened his mouth but no sound came out.

'Shock,' offered Shorty. 'Look over here, boss. What d'you think?'

He walked to the open long french doors leading out on to the narrow balcony. The boss glared at Compton then followed Shorty out on to the strip of paving. Eighteen floors down Monkton City went about its own way for enjoying the cool of the late evening. The two men peered down into the sea of twinkling lights, screwing up their eyes in an attempt to focus.

'H'm,' said the boss, slowly. 'Could be. Get down there. If your hunch is right, you know who to call. And tell that manager I want him up here if he knows what's good for him.'

Shorty bustled out. Compton had not moved. The boss sat down in a chair facing him, took out a slim gold case and extracted two cigarettes. He lit both, leaned across and tapped the other man on the knee.

'Here.'

He extended one of the cigarettes, a thin spiral of grey smoke curling round his outstretched fingers as he did so.

6

Compton jumped slightly, then took the cigarette and sucked greedily at it.

'I can see where this would be a shock, Mr. Compton,' said the boss. 'You don't get to murder somebody every day. But you better start talking, and real soon if we're gonna clean this up.' Compton shook his head, slowly at first, then gradually faster as if that gave the gesture added weight.

'No,' he finally managed, a strangled sound. Then his voice became clearer. 'No, no, you have this entirely wrong. Accident.'

Involuntarily his gaze swivelled round to the window. The boss noted this and was glad he'd despatched Shorty so promptly.

'Accident?' His voice was heavy with sarcasm. 'Just how did this accident happen, Mr. Compton?'

Compton was still shaking his head.

'Accident,' he repeated heavily. 'Just having a little fight that was all.'

'A little fight,' repeated the boss. 'That's murder, Compton.'

'No, really no,' protested the stout man.

7

'Wasn't even a serious fight, just kidding, you know. Least that's what I thought.

'Then suddenly it was getting serious. I'd had a lot to drink, you know that. I seemed to be losing my temper, and we were struggling over by the window, and then — '

'Then bingo,' said the boss. 'Next stop, the street level. Murder.'

His voice was harsh and it whipped into the frightened man like a lash.

'Don't say that,' he pleaded. 'It was an accident.'

'You were fighting,' repeated his interrogator. 'You were drunk. That's a case of drunken assault, did you know that?'

'Sure, well that's a long way from murder.' Some hint of confidence began to creep into Compton's voice. The boss listened to it with impatience.

'Drunken assault is a felony,' he said sharply. 'Now we have a dead body on our hands. The law says if life is taken during the commission of a felony, it's murder.'

'Sure, but that's not like this,' Compton's gain in confidence was oozing away

8

as he spoke. 'That's for guys who shoot guards when they're robbing a bank or something. That's not for ordinary people who — '

'Who do what? Tell me about you nice ordinary people. Tell me about how you get drunk, and fight with other nice ordinary people then wind up tossing them out of eighteenth storey windows. No don't tell me.' He jerked a red plastic telephone from a side table and threw it in Compton's lap. 'Tell the police. Just explain how it was and tell them you'll pay the fine.'

Compton had shrunk within himself again. He fingered nervously at the receiver.

'Number please,' said a small metallic voice. The receiver was dislodged from its cradle. 'Number please.'

With shaking fingers, the stout man broke the connection. The boss grinned, a mirthless expression.

'So you're beginning to get the idea.'

There was a tap at the door. Shorty walked in accompanied by an agitated man in a dark suit with a worried face beneath the grey hair.

'Well?' barked the boss.

The hotel manager began to speak.

'What is this nonsense I've been told — ' he started.

'Shut up,' snapped the other. 'Sit down there and wait. What'd you find?'

This was to Shorty, who nodded.

'What we thought. It's being cleaned up right now.'

He looked at Compton, who shivered.

'He don't look so good,' commented Shorty.

'Yeah,' agreed the boss. 'Get him a drink, a big one.'

Shorty turned his attention to the shining liquor cabinet which stood against one wall.

'I must say — ' began the manager.

'No you mustn't,' retorted the boss. 'You listen. When I'm through you can talk, not before. Now this man here, name of Compton, he just committed murder right here in this room.'

The manager blanched and looked quickly at Compton. A glance at the grey-faced shuddering man in the chair

10

gave him no consolation.

The boss went on talking. He talked for several minutes, and at the end of it the manager attempted to argue, but the attempt was little more than a formality. After a few more minutes he left. The boss turned back to Shorty.

'Get the Mex in here.'

Shorty went out, and was back in less than a minute. With him was a raven-haired girl of obvious Spanish extraction. The boss looked at her carefully.

'You tell her anything?' he demanded.

'You know I didn't,' replied Shorty.

It seemed to satisfy the questioner.

'All right, you can do something for me,' he told the girl.

'Anything, Meester — ' she began.

'Shut up and listen. This man here — ' he nodded at Compton — 'He's had a bad time. He's maybe a little delirious too. He needs to be looked after for a coupla days. I been watching you. You got a little more class than those other twists out there. Come from a good home, huh?'

'Oh yes, why my — '

11

'O.K. So you look after this guy. Just feed him, do whatever needs doing. There's an apartment at West Shore you can use. You do this right and keep your mouth shut, you get five hundred bucks, you hear? Five hundred dollars.'

'Five hundred dollars,' she repeated slowly, as if such a sum were a new conception.

'Sure. That's if you do it right.' His voice took on another tone. 'You do it wrong, you're gonna be sorry. Last year there was a dame kicked to death, right in this town. She used to work for me once. Catch?'

'I catch, señor.'

'All right, then do it.' He turned back to Shorty. 'Pick up this guy's stuff, all of it. Take him and the dame to the West Shore place and make sure they got everything they need. Then just get back here fast. If we're going to square this off we're gonna have a busy night.'

A few minutes later, if anybody at the party had been in the mood to look round, they would have seen a stout middle-aged man, who looked decidedly ill, leaving the apartment. He was leaning heavily on the arm of a slim, dark girl who was whispering to him softly. Behind the ill-assorted pair walked another younger man. He was carrying a grip, and seemed to be ushering the others on.

Not that anybody thought of looking round. The well-developed blonde was now performing a solo exhibition, a strip tease this time. The teasing was almost finished now, and the blonde only had one flimsy article of clothing left to remove.

Nobody looked round.

1

I'd been sitting around the office since nine a.m. and here it was almost eleven-thirty. Outside, the sun was steaming up the streets and there wasn't much traffic around. In Monkton City in early July people don't go in much for tearing around in the middle of the day. The only reasons that will get them out of their cool shady homes have to be business reasons. Nobody in town seemed to have found any business with me that would justify leaving the shade. I didn't blame them, and was mentally running over my list of cool shady bars when Florence Digby came in. She surveyed the polished surface of my empty desk with silent disapproval. Miss Digby looked cool and unflustered as always. The summer heat never gets the better of her, and the lemon-coloured suit looked as though she'd just put it on for the first time.

'The enquiry desk is on the line, Mr.

Preston,' she announced. 'They have a man down there who wishes to see you. As he is not exactly our usual type of client they asked me to check with you before letting him come up.'

The idea of having to exert myself did not appeal. I glowered.

'What kind of a man? What does he want?'

'He won't say. He says you're a private investigator and he's come for private reasons. Reasons he will not discuss with anyone else. He is a Mexican person.'

Miss Digby's grandmother was from Texas.

'Does he have a name?'

'Morales. According to the clerk at the desk the man is practically a hobo.'

That's the way it is in this business. Just when you think you might pass the time of day with a frosted glass, you have to sit around chewing the fat with a Mexican hobo who has private reasons. I toyed with the idea of sending him away, but I could see from Miss Digby's face she was expecting that.

'O.K., lets have a look at him.'

She looked surprised.

'You're going to see him?'

With a great show of patience I replied, 'I am going to see him. I wasn't at the Alamo, Miss Digby.'

She sniffed and went out. Now I was stuck with it. Just for the momentary satisfaction of making Florence Digby guess wrong I now had to follow through. A few minutes later she was back. Opening the door she stood well to one side and announced.

'Mr. Morales.'

I could see the point of view of the clerk at the enquiry desk. Mr. Morales was short and very dark-skinned, with thick black hair and a movie-villain moustache. Around fifty years old, his lined and furrowed face had the texture of old leather. Wrinkles were clustered thickly around his dark eyes, from years of squinting against the bright sun. He wore a pair of faded khaki pants and an old blue jacket on which there remained just one button. The jacket was tied around his middle with a length of twine. His gnarled hands picked nervously at the brim of an unbelievably ancient straw hat.

'How do you do, Mr. Morales. Come on in and sit down.'

He grinned nervously, frowned, then advanced a tentative pace into the room. It was far enough to permit Florence Digby to get the door closed, which she did with a firm click. Morales whipped around apprehensively, and was evidently relieved to see the last of his escort.

'Señor Preston?'

The voice was pleasant.

'The same. Please sit down.'

This time he did, perching dangerously on the extreme edge of the visitor's chair. He was so ill-at-ease I half-expected him to get up and run out of the door.

'Hot today,' I offered.

He nodded unhappily. Then, as if his mind was suddenly made up, he plunged a hand inside the dusty blue jacket and came out with a brown paper parcel. This he placed on the table in front of me, tapping at it with his index finger for emphasis.

'One hundred dollars,' he informed me. 'You find Juanita for me. Yes?'

'Hold on, Mr. Morales. Let's take it a little slower. Who is Juanita?'

'Who? She is my Juanita. My little one.' He banged himself on the chest.

'Ah. Your daughter?'

'Si. Daughter. You will find her please, señor?'

'Perhaps. First, some questions.'

I took a clean white notepad from a drawer, picked up a pen. Morales watched this performance with marked approval. This was more like it. This made it official. I could practically hear him thinking. When a man sits behind a desk it is right he should make writing on paper. Bueno.

'Now, what is your full name, please.'

'Ramon Estaban Morales.'

I wrote that down. Evidently if I wanted to know what it was Morales had come about, the question and answer method was the best way to find out.

'Where do you live?'

He looked puzzled.

'Your home,' I asked.

'Ah, si. I live in Punta Felipe. It is near San Francisco.'

19

I don't claim to know every whistle stop in the state, but I'd never heard of a place near San Francisco by that name.

'Punta Felipe,' I repeated slowly as I wrote it down. 'Don't seem to call it to mind, Mr. Morales. Which way out from San Francisco does it lie?'

He was worried again.

'Which way? From San Francisco, Señor Preston, there is only one road to the coast. My village is at the other end of the road. It is thirty kilometers journey.'

'One road to the coast? What is this, some kind of gag?'

'Señor?'

He sat on the edge of the chair watching me unhappily. If it was a gag he meant to stick it out to the end. I jerked my thumb at the large-scale map that hangs on the office wall.

'O.K., Mr. Morales. Would you mind pointing out Punta Felipe on that map?'

Anxious to please, he scuttled across to the map, stared at it, tut-tutted and shook his head.

'So sorry,' he said, eyeing me with apprehension. 'On this map there are many names. How could I find my village?'

'If it's near San Francisco it ought to be easy. Every community larger than one hundred people is entered on that map. Every place in the State of California.'

He nodded as I spoke, and seemed to be struggling mentally. Finally he smiled triumphantly.

'California? The United States? But I am not from here, señor. My village is in Baja California. Mexico.'

If it hadn't been such a hot morning I'd have been a little quicker on the ball. I went across and stood beside him. Sure enough, about one third of the way down the slender peninsula was San Francisco. I put a finger on it and turned to Morales.

'There it is, Mr. Morales.'

He practically embraced me. When we were sitting down again I got back to the questions.

'You're a long way from home. About three hundred miles, I should guess. You didn't come all that way just to see me?'

'To see you, señor. Si. I think you find my Juanita.'

21

Sincerity leaked out all over the man.

'How'd you come to have my name?' I queried.

'From the newspaper. Juanita she sends all the time the Americano newspaper. I read much of you. You kill this hombre, Toreno.[1] You are a friend of thees millionaire Señor Freeman. You are very high-class.'

What Marsland Freeman II would say if he heard that, I chuckled to think.

'You could have written a letter,' I suggested.

'A letter? I wish to ask a high-class man like you to find out what has happened to my beautiful Juanita, and I write a letter? Oh, no, señor. I come here, to this place. I see you, talk with you. This is not something of which to write the letters.'

I digested that. Then, pointing to the money.

'One hundred dollars is a lot of money, Mr. Morales. Not every man in Punta Felipe could find such a sum I imagine?'

'Si, you are right.' He heaved his

---

[1] *Murder is for Keeps.*

shoulders sadly. 'For thees money I have made many promises. But it is no matter, if my Juanita is safe. I, Ramon Estaban Morales, am a man of honour. The promises will be kept. I shall not complain.'

I found myself curious about the promises. A hundred dollars American, was probably more than Morales and his whole family had to live on in a year. Still, it wasn't any of my business. Not yet.

'Tell me about Juanita,' I prompted.

'Ah, Juanita.' He nodded and smiled. 'I have three daughters, señor. Two of these are like other village girls. They work hard, they respect their mother, they listen to Father Tomaso.'

'But not the other one? Not Juanita?'

He sighed.

'Not Juanita. My other girls, they are nice girls, pretty girls. My Juanita, she is not only pretty. She has a fire, a hot blood. She is more beautiful than the sunrise. I tell myself she is young. In time she will settle her mind, she will become as the others.'

'But it didn't work out that way. She

wanted to come to the States, get ahead in the world?'

'Not at first. At the mission school, Juanita had a friend, Isabella Martinez. She is a wild one. Not beautiful like my Juanita, but one the men want, just the same. Isabella go to San Francisco one day for her father. She does not come back. Then a letter comes. Isabella is a grand lady here in Monkton City. She send money, much money, to her father.'

'What was she doing that brought in all the money?' I asked.

'I do not know, señor. But Isabella, she was a wild one. After she is gone my Juanita becomes very quiet. I think to myself, this is good. The wild one has left the village, now my Juanita will come back to her family. How little we know, señor.'

He looked at me, sadness written wide in the dark eyes. I'd heard the story before, hundreds of times, and I didn't see any reason why this one should end any more happily than they usually do. But I couldn't help feeling sorry for this bewildered little man. Gently, I prodded him on.

'What happened then?'

'One day Juanita left to teach at the school like any other day. Only she didn't go to the mission, she went to San Francisco and came straight here. I tried to follow her, but it was almost ten hours before we were sure she'd gone. It was no use.'

'How long ago did all this happen?'

'Five months now. After two weeks, she write a letter. She has a fine position in Monkton City. She earns much money, and some she sends to me, her father. We rejoice, señor. Our little girl has not become a bad girl. Perhaps I do not understand her. Perhaps she is right, our village was not the place for such a one as Juanita.'

Morales refused a cigarette. I lit one, and watched the grey smoke hang lazily in the air.

'About this fine position she had. Did she ever tell you any more about that?'

'Ah, si. She was personal maid to a fine lady. Mrs. Floyd Whitton Junior. She live in a fine house with many rooms — '

'Yes, I know about Mrs. Whitton,' I

assured him. 'So Juanita was working there and everything was fine. What happened then?'

'A month ago, she disappear. I have no letter from her, so I write. My letter come back from the house, and they say she has left them. Since then I have heard nothing.'

'I see.'

For one hundred dollars I was supposed to find a beautiful girl in Monkton City. A girl who didn't want to be found. With ten experienced men I might cover the whole City in six months. Of course there was nothing to say Juanita had settled for Monkton. It took only thirty minutes on the inter-state bus to make Los Angeles, and, what with the boom and all, that gave me an extra four million people to sift through. After that there was the rest of California, and all those other little real-estate lots that made up the United States of America. For a hundred bucks it looked like a lot of work.

'Have you been to the house? Mrs. Whitton's house, I mean?'

'Ah, señor, no,' Morales was horrified. 'How could I disgrace my Juanita in thees fashion? She have a fine position at that house. What will the lady think to see such as I?'

He waved a hand expressively over his clothes. The poor little guy was right. The Whittons would have set the dogs on him long before he made the front door. The unfairness of it nettled me.

'Mr. Morales, I want to tell you the truth,' I said slowly. 'I don't know whether I can find your daughter. This is a big town, and there's a much bigger one nearby. But I will try. I will ask some questions, visit some places, I will try. Remember that I guarantee nothing.'

He jerked his head up and down. With the flowing moustache the whole effect was like one of those Mardi Gras masks.

He pushed himself a little further back into the chair. Evidently my client was going to move in until I'd produced his daughter.

'It may take a while,' I told him. 'Where can I reach you?'

'Ah.' He shot up and stood in front of

the desk. 'I come back later.'

He made as if to walk out but I called him back.

'One moment. Have you a picture of Juanita? One I could borrow for a while?'

'I have it.'

Morales plunged a brown hand inside the gaping jacket again. When he brought it out he was holding a small photograph. He handed it over. Two dark-haired girls in white dresses were standing self-consciously in front of a church. The picture was taken from too far back to enable anyone to get a close look at the faces.

'Very nice,' I said. 'Which one is — ?'

He leaned across and tapped at the figure on the right of the picture.

'Juanita,' he explained. 'She was fifteen years old.'

'And the other?'

'The wild one. Isabella Martinez.'

I looked with some interest at wild Isabella. She didn't look especially wild to me. But then, who can tell?'

'How old is Juanita now?'

'Nineteen. Last week she is nineteen.'

Fine. To help locate a nineteen-year old I had a badly-printed long-shot of her, taken four years earlier.

'How about Isabella, Mr. Morales? Any address that you know of?'

He shook his head.

'Her father, he no tell me, and I do not ask. That Martinez,' he shrugged, 'So long as he can have his wine and his tobacco, I do not believe he cares about his Isabella.'

'Uh huh. Tell me, have you been to the police about all this?'

'Police.' His eyes almost rolled round full circle. 'Ah señor, this is a matter of great confidence, but I do not think the police help me. Or my Juanita. We have no papers.'

If a Mexican wishes to cross the border into the U.S. he has to have his papers in order. Particularly if he wants to stay and work like Juanita had.

'If you haven't any papers, how did you cross the border? The trains are always inspected.'

'I do not come by train, señor. For this a man must pay many dollars. I have no dollars, except the money which I must

29

pay to the señor for him to find Juanita.'

'Then how did you get here?' I pressed.

'I walk,' he replied simply. 'Sometimes a kind person permits me to ride in a wagon. Once I ride inside a very fine automobile. But most of the time I walk.'

If I was caught helping a border-hopping immigrant, I'd lose not only my licence but also several months of my freedom. But when a man walks a good part of three hundred miles to see me, I figure he's entitled to a little service. I tried to impress on Morales that if he were questioned by the police he wasn't to mention my name, and finally I was satisfied that he had the idea. Then I thought of Pop Kline. If I persuaded him to keep Morales off the street for a day or so it might improve my chances of staying in business. Leaving Morales in my office, I went through to Florence Digby and asked her to get Pop on the line. I'd been able to help him out a few months back when a couple of loud mouths tried to sell him the protection gag. He promised me anything, any time. Well, this was the time. I talked with him on the telephone, and he said he'd come up right away to collect Morales. I went back inside.

'A friend of mine is on the way here,' I informed him. 'You will stay with him for now.'

'Ah but señor, I cannot pay,' he protested. 'This cost plenty dinero, and I cannot — '

I flagged him down.

'You have already paid,' I assured him, waving towards the brown paper parcel. 'The fee is inclusive. While I work on the case, you will remain with my friend, eat with him. It is the custom.'

And that sold him. People from the other side of the border are much too proud to take charity, as a rule. But a custom was a different matter entirely.

'Ah, si. The custom,' he nodded with satisfaction.

While we waited for Pop Kline I did my best to get some kind of a description of Juanita, but all I wound up with was a lot of flowery description that a Hollywood press agent would not have dared hand out. Fifteen minutes later Pop arrived and took charge of my client. I managed to convey to Pop that he was to keep

31

Morales tucked out of sight as much as possible. Then they left together and I had the office back to normal again.

Well, not quite. On the table was a tattered parcel containing one hundred dollars. Somewhere outside the shimmering windows was a nineteen year old illegal immigrant named Juanita Morales. I had to find her, and I wasn't going to do that from inside.

Regretfully, I tossed the money in a drawer, and made for the door.

2

On my way out to the Whitton place I thought about the family history. Floyd Whitton Senior hit Monkton City in 1894. In his pocket he had two dollars and thirty-seven cents, so the story goes. He was twenty-three years old, strong and ambitious. The gold fever was rife in the Monkton air, and a man had to be young and strong just to stay healthy. The same night he arrived he came across a pack of toughies baiting an old man named Bonanza Charlie. Whitton sent the hoodlums on their way and bought the old man supper with the last of his money. Charlie was a well-known local butt, who claimed to have found half the gold in the States at one time or another. Being inexperienced, young Whitton agreed to accompany the old man on his latest search. They spent three fruitless months looking for the rich vein Bonanza Charlie talked about. Then they came back to Monkton City, and went their ways. Later Whitton was told the old man was dying and wanted to see him. Bonanza Charlie was dying all right, and he gave Whitton a roll of buffalo leather. Charlie claimed the writing on it was a land grant made out to him by War Horse, Eagle Chief of the Techapi, the local Indian tribe. Charlie had saved War Horse's brother from a hanging party, and in return the chief gave him a small piece of hunting land, twenty miles by ten. The old man had never forgotten that Whitton had been good to him, and he left a will, properly witnessed, leaving all his possessions to Whitton, including the land grant. Bonanza Charlie died that night, Whitton shoved the worthless land grant in his poke and forgot about it.

Later, he struck up an acquaintance with a young lawyer named Ephraim Pattison. During an idle conversation one evening he mentioned his status as a landowner, half in fun. Pattison was interested, wanted to see the buffalo hide. It didn't take a trained legal mind long to see the possibilities. Pattison went to the

State Capitol. When he came back Whitton found himself the recognised owner of that small piece of land. Only it wasn't hunting land any more. Small industries had sprung up in some parts of it. Whitton began to cash in, and left to himself he'd probably have sold out his entire interest for a few hundred dollars. But Pattison was there, cajoling, steadying, negotiating. Within five years Whitton was a millionaire, still with a large part of his land undeveloped. Pattison faded out at the turn of the century but Whitton had learned enough by then. He became bigger all the time. When the war over in Europe got under way, Whitton was estimated to be worth eight million dollars. By the time he'd made his contribution to the war effort the cash register was reading seventeen million. He built a hospital, a school, a sports ground, another school. He seemed to be giving all his money away, but like so many of these philanthropists the more he gave away the richer he got.

All this time he remained a bachelor. Then at the age of fifty-six he suddenly married Louise Brighten, daughter of one of his business associates, and thirty years his junior. At the same time he announced his retirement from active business. It was 1927. Whitton cashed in for twenty-five million dollars, and the big crash two years later couldn't touch him. Louise bore him four children, three boys and a girl. When he died at the age of eighty-two, Monkton City had a public day of mourning. Half the buildings in town bore his name, there was a memorial erected in Whitton Square the following year. Every citizen in town felt a sense of personal loss at the passing of this man who had affected the daily lives of everyone.

Every citizen, that is, but the Whitton children. Till that time they had all been models of the kind of behaviour people expect from royalty. Once the old man died, they seemed to go wild. They were all filthy rich as individuals, as well as a family, and they seemed to be making an effort to get rid of their money just as fast as they could.

All this went through my mind as I

headed for the Whitton house on Palm Lake Canyon. Floyd Whitton Jnr. was the eldest of the brood and would be in his early thirties now. I knew very little about him, beyond the fact that he'd married a blues singer he picked up in a joint on the Strip, about four years earlier. I'd heard plenty about her at the time. The name she used in those days was Dixie Brown, and it's probably as good as any other. Nobody had been able to trace where Dixie Brown came from, but after a time that didn't seem so important. What was important was that she was the wife of Floyd Whitton Jnr., and her odd conceptions of the behaviour expected of her made plenty of copy for the local newshawks. If they ever had any spare ink, they could be sure Dixie Whitton was good for a column or two. Like the time she gave a party at eleven in the morning. The guests had to wear evening dress, and arrive on ostriches. No ostrich, no in. And getting in to a Whitton party was just as important today as ever it was. Only the reasons were different, and so was the guest list.

I pulled in outside the white-painted iron gates and pressed the horn. A character dressed up like a cop appeared behind the gates and looked through at me. He was a youngish man, with a built-in scowl which marred his otherwise good-looking face.

'Whom did you wish to see, sir?'

The 'sir' was a pointed insult. I grinned, my open boyish grin.

'I'm calling on Mrs. Whitton, friend. On a personal matter. A very personal matter. If you like the job, better get the gates open.'

I made a personal matter sound like the kind of matter he'd understand. There was little doubt about what interpretation he would put on it. Not unless he didn't know much about Dixie Whitton. He sighed, unlocked the gates and swung them open.

'I'll telephone the house you're coming up. What name, sir?'

He gave me the 'sir' again.

'Preston. Mark Preston,' I told him. 'I'll tell Mrs. Whitton you didn't keep me waiting, friend.'

He shrugged and walked over to a small building beside the gate, presumably to telephone the house. I eased between the gates and rolled around the wide sweeping curve of the white-kerbed drive. The palm trees had been planted by Floyd Whitton Snr. He'd paid some guy to come all the way from New York to plan the layout of the gardens in front of the house. The palms had been spaced out cunningly, so that they presented a solid screen from the roadway, giving the impression of a small forest. In fact there were only a few rows of trees, and behind them lay the famous Whitton lawns. Acres of lush green velvet, where a weed would have shouted aloud, like a red coat at a Fourth of July parade. I could see the house now, a middle Californian horror, with Spanish curves and archways, Eastern turrets and minarets, all scattered indiscriminately around a central squat ugliness of reactionary red brick. To ensure that the building commanded the eye the architect, long since gone to face a higher judgment, had thrown up a huge mound, a kind of earthwork, and dumped his house on top. To me it looked for all the world like a vast cake, on which some demented baker had stuck too much decoration. The deep white steps leading up to the doors were strictly from the South. Here you could almost see the young bucks lounging elegantly around, trying to impress Miss Cindy Lou, unaware of the storm clouds gathering over the old plantation etc. I made good time up the steps, careful to see I didn't trip over my sword. At the top stood a large coloured man. He was dressed like a butler, but he also looked capable of arranging my return down the steps if I got out of line.

'Mr. Preston, sir?'

The voice was deep and pleasant. It had more the feeling of an actor's delivery than a butler's. I fished around for a card. He took it, stared at it unimpressed, then dropped it onto a small silver tray he'd been hiding behind his back.

'Like to see Mrs. Whitton on a personal matter, if she can spare me a few moments,' I told him.

'This way, please.'

I followed him into the house. He showed me into a small room leading off the hall.

'If you will please wait, I'll see if my mistress is at home.'

That was a nice touch. Plenty of people would have said 'if she will see you'. This guy said 'if she's at home'. Not much, a small thing, but a nice touch. Then he could bounce me with no hard feelings either side. As it happened it wasn't necessary. Within a short time he came back into the room.

'If you will please follow me.'

The stroll down the hall would have been bad news for anybody with an upset stomach. The suits of armour had all been filled with wax dummies and placed in set action pieces. I guess fighting in those days was a serious matter, but I'd sooner read about it than see it. Some lay on the floor, split in two by axes, others merely had lances or arrows stuck through their middles. One decapitated body lay in a mess of realistic gore. I shuddered.

'I guess you can get used to anything,' I muttered.

'Sir?'

'The dummies,' I explained. 'Gory sense of humour somebody has.'

'Oh. When I first came here I had nightmares. But as you say, sir, one gets used to anything.'

He smiled. He had a pleasant smile, with two magnificent rows of teeth to back it up. We were out of the hall now, stepping through glass doors leading out on to a terrace at the back of the house.

'Mr. Preston, madam.'

The polite negro withdrew. There was one of those lounging sun-chairs placed with its back to the house. A woman's head was just visible at one end.

'C'mon over here, let's get a look at you.'

This voice was deep too, but for pleasantness I'd take the butler's. I walked across the patterned marble and around the side of the chair. Sprawled full length was the woman I'd come to see, Dixie Whitton. She had long, slim brown legs and a tight, flat stomach. Firm high breasts merged into her smooth golden brown shoulders. Tousled black hair hung carelessly over one side of her face. She had soft grey eyes, with a perfect nose and lips a little too generous for the small face. She wore no make-up, just lipstick, and she didn't need any. There was one thin strip of black shiny material stretched tightly over her lower half, and another even thinner, which was losing the battle to restrain her bosom. She looked at me with lazy interest.

'Thought you were a private eye?'

'That's right, Mrs. Whitton,' I confirmed.

'Aren't you supposed to wear a raincoat?'

She reached down with her right hand, groping for the glass that stood beside the chair.

'I do have a raincoat,' I assured her. 'If you're disappointed I'll go home and put it on.'

'Never mind. Doesn't matter.'

She took a noisy gulp at the pink stuff in the glass. Judging from the glazed appearance of her eyes, she wasn't going to need much more of that today.

'Drink?' she demanded suddenly.

'Yes. I drink,' I admitted.

'Didn't mean that. Meant d'you wanna drink now? Hey,' she looked shocked, 'Hey you knew what I meant.'

'I knew what you meant,' I nodded.

I walked across to a glass-topped cane table with several bottles on it, and checked the labels. They covered a weird assortment of rare liqueurs and high proof-content imported spirits. Mrs. Whitton watched as I walked back to her.

'Mind if I sit down?'

There was a shaped piece of wood that could just have been a chair. She nodded.

'Help yourself, Mr. — ?'

'Preston,' I supplied. 'Mark Preston. It was on the card.'

'Was it?' She didn't seem interested, 'Hey, you didn't take a drink.'

'Have to watch my stomach,' I said, easily. 'It's only conditioned to whisky. Preferably Scotch. That stuff over there is strictly for he-men.'

She thought about that. The glass of pink stuff was still in her hand. Now she held it up against the sunlight and twirled it in her fingers.

'He-men, huh? Where does that leave me? Guess it makes me a he-gal — no, that can't be right. A she-man.' She looked at me, almost anxiously. 'A she-man? You think that's what you'd call me?'

What I would probably have called her on my own time was a different affair. At the moment I was on Ramon Estaban Morales' time, and he didn't have a lot to spare.

'From where I'm sitting I'll give you fifty per cent of that, Mrs. Whitton. You're only half-right. You look all she to me.'

She chuckled.

'The words. You do have the words, Preston. That's what I miss sometimes. These characters we get coming to the house. Oh, they're not bad. Not so bad anyway, some of 'em. But they don't know the words.'

'Just hum the tune, Mrs. Whitton. Once I got the key I'll be able to follow you.'

She made an effort to concentrate on me. I hoped the result was worth the facial contortions she put into it.

'You sure you're a private cop?' she demanded.

'I'm sure.'

'You ever been in the music business?'

'No, ma'am. Just a hardworking investigator.'

'H'mph,' she commented. 'What tune do you want to hear, anyway?'

'Do you know the one about a little Mexican girl named Juanita?'

As I spoke I was trying to catch any expression that might appear on her face when the name was mentioned. Fear, doubt, panic, take your choice. I got a nil reaction.

'Juanita? Not that Morales girl again? What about her now?' She looked like somebody about to get bored.

'She seems to have gone missing, Mrs. Whitton. Her father is worried about her. I've been retained to see if I can find her.'

'Don't see what I can do,' she grumbled. 'Kid wasn't here long. Came around — oh — middle of February, I guess. She was a pretty one, real good-looker. You know dark hair, flashing eyes, all that jazz? She seemed to like it here well enough. Then one day she was gone. Just like that. End of story.'

'Thank you. You won't mind if I fill in with a question or two?'

'Help yourself. All it takes is time. Time, I got in barrels, Mr. Preston.'

'How did Miss Morales come to get the job with you?'

'Does it matter?'

'It might.'

'Somebody knew I was looking for a new girl. Er'm — just a minute, yes. It was Gregg. Gregg Hudson, you know him?'

'No. What would Mr. Hudson's interest be, exactly?'

She laughed. I thought there was a bitter note in there somewhere.

'His interest? Brother, you really don't know Gregg. He only has the one interest that I'm aware of — women. All kinds, all shapes, all sizes.'

'Sounds like a busy man,' I commented. 'Where would I find him?'

'I've no idea. Gregg likes to move around a lot. 'Phone company could tell you, I guess.'

'Thank you. While she was working here, did Miss Morales have any special

47

friends you know of? Any organisation she belonged to, stuff like that?'

She pondered for a moment. As the conversation progressed, Dixie Brown Whitton was gradually sobering up. Whether that was good or bad from my point of view I'd have to wait and find out.

'Not that I knew of. She had her free time, naturally. All day off on a Thursday, most of Sunday if I didn't need her. And she'd be able to go out most any evening after about nine. Where she went I didn't ask.'

'I see. The day she disappeared, what happened?'

'Nothing happened, she just cut out.'

I could sense my hostess had had about enough of me, and my questions. But I wasn't quite finished yet.

'I mean did she say she was leaving then pack a bag and go? Or did she leave early in the morning before anybody got up, or what?'

'Yeah, that's it. The last one, I mean. One morning she was gone. She helped me get ready to go out the night before, same as usual. Next morning she wasn't there.'

'Just now, you said she was free most evenings after nine o'clock. If you went out on this particular evening, couldn't it have been that she left soon after you?'

'I guess so. Does it make any difference?'

'It could.' I wondered whether I could risk one more question. Mrs. Whitton looked as though she might be getting set to have me thrown out. 'When we started talking about her, you said I wasn't the first person to ask about Miss Morales.'

'I said that?' She cocked her head to one side.

'Something like it. When I mentioned her name you said, 'Not that Morales girl again'.'

'So?'

'So who else has been asking about her?'

She sighed and stretched. It was midday in a hot July and whatever else you may hear about me, I'm only human. If she did that again I might find myself in some real expensive trouble. When she

49

didn't answer I thought for a moment she'd fallen asleep. Then she opened one eye and looked at me pensively.

'What do you weigh, Preston?'

'Hundred and eighty-eight,' I told her.

'I would have said a little more.'

'It's the coat,' I explained. 'Like a loose coat in this weather. Who else asked about Juanita Morales?'

'Gregg did. 'Phoned me up a couple of days after she walked out.'

'Why was he interested? And how did he know she was gone?'

'Didn't till he 'phoned. Then he wanted to know all about it. Satisfied?'

'Thank you.'

I stood up.

'You're not leaving, are you?'

'Yes. You've been very helpful and I want to thank you.'

'Brother Preston, you ain't seen nothing yet. Floor show goes on in just a few minutes.'

She swung her legs down off the lounging chair and sat upright. The movement gave the two thin strips that passed for a bathing suit plenty of action.

From where I was sitting the floor show was already on.

'I think the cover charge might come a little high for me,' I said.

She chuckled. Then she stood up and came across to where I was standing. She leaned against me heavily, her fingers idling around on my back. I had to put my arms around her to prevent her falling, at least that's what I told myself. Her flesh was smooth and yielding. I decided I could risk the cover charge after all. She felt the reaction in me and laughed softly into my shoulder. Then she dropped her head back and closed her eyes swaying gently in my arms. Her teeth were sharp and the fingers in my back became nails. She broke first, opening the grey eyes and looking up at me with a mocking smile.

'We have a special offer today. No charge to any private eye weighing a hundred and eighty-eight pounds.'

'This must be the place,' I replied.

Then she stepped back and looked me up and down carefully.

'In a week you'll be lucky if you tip a

hundred and sixty.'

'I'll take a chance,' I told her.

She picked up her now empty glass and held it out to me.

'There's no hurry, lover. We have all the time in the world. Pour me a drink, huh?'

I took the glass and went back to the table. As far as I was able to judge my hand was trembling. I identified the bottle by the obnoxious colour of the content. The lady was drinking some unpronounceable stuff that was brought in from Turkey. As I started to pour the drink there was a sudden cough from the glass doors. I almost jumped out of my skin.

The negro butler stood there. I wished I could guess how long he'd been there.

'Well?' snapped Dixie.

'The master has telephoned, madam. Jackson has just left to pick him up at the station. He will be home in about twenty minutes.'

Then he withdrew. Dixie stood quite still biting at her lower lip with those sharp teeth.

'Damn,' she said softly. 'Damn, damn, damn.'

She took a vicious kick at the chair I'd been sitting in.

'Said he wouldn't be home till Saturday. I know why he's doing this. I know his filthy little ways.'

I handed her the drink. Without a word she took it and poured it straight down. It would have corroded the plates on a battleship, but she poured it away like water. Then she grinned.

'You said if I hummed the tune you'd follow.'

'That's right. We seem to have got off-key.'

I went to the doorway, ready to leave.

'Hey, Preston.'

I waited. She stood in the sunlight, the golden brown body gleaming.

'You'll call me, huh?'

'I'll call you.'

In the hall the butler was hovering around, expecting me to turn up.

'You're leaving, sir?'

'Yes.'

He made a short bowing movement

from the waist and led the way to the top of the white stone steps.

'Good afternoon, Mr. Preston.'

'Good afternoon.'

I could feel him watching me all the way down. At the bottom I turned and looked at the still upright figure against the background of that architectural nightmare. I tried a half-wave, but drew no response.

The inside of the car was like an oven as I headed back into town.

3

After I'd eaten a couple of sandwiches
and swallowed a glass of milk
downtown, I set out to find Gregg
Hudson. People often overlook the
simple method of getting information.
Often, the only trouble you need take if
you want to find out something is to go
to the city library. There they have all
kinds of reference books, directories and
such. All you have to do is walk in the
door and start reading. My first try for
Hudson didn't even need that much
effort. I simply looked in the 'phone
directory. We ran to six Hudson G.s in
Monkton. I stacked up with change and
went to work. The first man I tried was
the manager of a progressive funeral
parlour. His name wasn't Gregg, it was
George, but he was anxious to talk to
me just the same. The gap in my life
apparently, was my omission to ensure
myself a comfortable and tasteful

journey into the hereafter. In my business, that's a topic I don't care to dwell on too much. The second was a Gerald Hudson and he wasn't the right man either. It was hot in the booth, and I leaned wearily against the side while the burring noise told me my third number was ringing. Finally there was a click and a man's voice said,

'Who is this?'

'Mr. Hudson?'

'Yeah. Who're you?'

'My name is Preston. Are you by any chance Mr. Gregg Hudson?'

There was a pause.

'My name is Gilbert Hudson. There is nobody by that name at this number?'

I had a feeling I was warm.

'You're sure you don't know the name?' I pressed.

'I didn't say that. What is this, some giveaway programme?'

'No,' I replied. 'I'm very anxious to get in touch with Gregg Hudson. It's important.'

He thought about that.

'You a bill-collector or something?'

From his tone he rather hoped I was a bill-collector.

'Something,' I told him.

He chuckled.

'You're out of luck. He's busted. He's always busted.'

'So you do know him?'

'Know him? I'm his brother. You know, there's always a brother. The one who does all the work. The one with a steady job. I'm that one.'

'I see. Do you know where I can find your brother, Mr. Hudson?'

'Not for sure. He moves around all the time. Haven't seen him in a couple of weeks. He was staying at the Venice Apartments then.'

I knew the place. A run-down block of apartments at the crumbling end of town.

'I'm much obliged for the information, Mr. Hudson.' I meant it.

'You're welcome. If you see him tell him — '

He stopped talking. I waited. After a moment or two,

'Tell him what, Mr. Hudson?' I prompted.

'Nothing, it doesn't matter. The Venice Apartments.'

He hung up. I wondered briefly what it was I wasn't to tell Gregg after all. From the way Gilbert Hudson spoke, he had no great regard for his brother.

I took a ride round to the Venice Apartments. In the strong sunshine, the shabby exterior looked even more faded than usual. Before the place started downhill there'd been a desk and a clerk to deal with visitors. The desk remained, silent witness to whatever went on in better days. There was no clerk. I stood in the gloomy entrance hall wondering which of the peeled paint doors was concealing Gregg Hudson.

'Somethin' you want, mister?'

An old man shuffled in from a side door. He was dressed in a shirt and pants of a uniform dirty grey. Two days growth of white stubble sprouted on his beaten face, and he was stooped almost double. The rheumy eyes wandered uncertainly over me, darting away at any suggestion that I might look straight at him. He scratched nervously at his armpit. An unappetising odour followed him from the open door.

'Calling on Mr. Gregg Hudson,' I told him. 'Can't remember the number.'

'Oh.'

He peered at me suspiciously, but otherwise remained quite still. I tried a second time.

'Do you know which room he's in?'

He shook his head slowly.

'Can't seem to recall,' he muttered. 'You know how it is, so many rooms so many people. Just can't seem to recall.'

He rubbed his hands together, licking his lips.

'You oughta take something for that memory,' I told him. 'Try this.'

I held out two dollar bills. He wiped one hand against the filthy shirt before taking the money. He nodded several times in rapid succession.

'That helps,' he cackled. 'It's comin' back fast. Real fast. Eight.'

Half of a broken figure '2' was skewed at a crazy angle on one of the doors. The rest were bare.

'Fine. Now just tell me which is eight and I'm all set.'

The old man was halfway through the doorway he'd emerged from. Now he paused, looked back at me.

'Upstairs,' he snapped. 'First onna right.'

I nodded and made my way up. There were no numbers on the doors upstairs either, but I had information from the guide. As I knocked at the door somebody turned down a radio inside the room.

'Who is it?'

A man's voice, not very interested in who it was.

'Mr. Hudson? Like a word with you,' I said to the closed door.

'What about?' he demanded.

'Kind of personal,' I replied. 'How about opening the door?'

'It's open. Help yourself.'

I turned the handle and the door swung inwards. A large man sat in a deep chair by the window. By his side was a table with a drawer open. One arm rested negligently on the table, fingers close above the open drawer. I didn't have to be Einstein to know he didn't keep his spare pocket handkerchiefs in the drawer. Gregg Hudson was broad-shouldered, tall as far as I could judge. His face was open and pleasant, except for a certain lack of frankness about the eyes. His hair was brown and curly and there was plenty of it. He wore a white silk sport shirt open at the neck, and a pair of well-cut slacks. He was taking a good look at me, too. I would have turned to shut the door, but didn't want to turn my back on those twitching fingers.

'Are you Gregg Hudson, a friend of Mrs. Whitton?'

He smiled, a nice wide toothpasty smile.

'That what she says?'

'Mr. Hudson, I'm not interested in Mrs. Whitton — ' I began.

'Ha ha,' he sneered. 'Why? You're not a fairy are you?'

I swallowed hard but felt the sudden hotness behind my ears and knew they'd turned red.

'I didn't come here to call names,

Hudson,' I said slowly.

'Brother, I don't care why you came here. I'm not interested. You can drop down real dead, right now.'

And he smiled again. If I lost my temper I'd get nowhere fast. At least I'd learned that much over the years.

'I don't get it,' I told him. 'Why do you want to be so tough to get along with?'

'Why should I want to get along with you?' he jeered. 'To me you're nothing, brother.'

'Then why don't you take your hand away from that drawer? Stand up where I can reach you, and stop hiding behind a few ounces of iron.'

He laughed quickly, made a sudden decision. With one movement he flipped the drawer shut and jumped to his feet.

'So you can reach me,' he scoffed. 'Now what are you going to do?'

I shrugged.

'Just ask a couple of questions, then blow. That's all I came here for.'

'Yeah?' he didn't sound too convinced. 'You're trouble, brother. You're a lawyer or a cop or you represent somebody.

Something like all that. You're trouble, whatever.'

'The name is Preston. I'm trying to find a girl who's gone missing. The family hired me.'

He breathed heavily.

'It figures. So why all that flumdum about Dixie? You tell me she's missing I'm going to call you a liar.'

'Mrs. Whitton was my first call. She thought maybe you could help me. The girl I'm looking for is Juanita Morales.'

Up till that point he'd been leaning forward very slightly, ready to start slugging any moment. Now he slumped back on his heels looking very surprised.

'The little Mex? What about her?'

'That's what I'm trying to find out. Do you know where she is?'

He looked puzzled, pulled at his left ear with a well-kept hand.

'This on the level? I mean about you trying to find her?'

'Sure. Why else would I be here?'

He laughed shortly.

'Never mind that now. Shut the door and sit down someplace.'

He turned away and helped himself to a cigarette from a pack that lay on top of the softly-playing radio. It was a complete change of front, but it was an improvement. I pushed the door shut, found myself a chair and parked.

'Preston, did you say?'

I nodded.

'I've heard the name somewheres.'

It was an invitation.

'Sometimes, if I'm unlucky on a caper, my name gets a little play in the paper.'

'Is that right? Good or bad play?' His interest was almost friendly.

'It depends what sheet you read. Sometimes I'm the well-known private investigator, sometimes I'm a guy it's time the police did something about.'

He nodded, suddenly clicked his fingers.

'Got you. You got a green light from Marsland Freeman in person a while back. Say, that Lois is quite a dish, huh?'

I didn't want to talk about Lois Freeman. Not to this character.

'She's a great person,' I confirmed. 'Now can I ask you about Juanita?'

'Oh, sure. Sure, go ahead.'

He was back in the chair by the window again. All the tension was gone from him, and he was now completely at his ease. Whatever he'd been expecting, whatever trouble was due, it wasn't a few questions about Juanita Morales.

'Mrs. Whitton told me you steered Juanita her way when she was looking for a personal maid. That true?'

'Sure. The kid needed a job. I knew Dixie had just lost a maid so I took the little Mex out there. No harm, is there?'

I ignored that.

'How'd you come to meet her?'

'Damned if I know. You know how it is, meet a few girls most any day. Nothing special I can remember about Juanita.'

He scratched at his head, thinking.

'They tell me you're quite a hand with the ladies,' I offered. The friendliness dissipated.

'You come here to talk about me or this wetback?' he demanded.

I made a note of the word wetback.

'No offence,' I assured him. 'My description of Juanita says she's quite a looker. I guess I was just thinking it must be the life when a man gets to meet a few girls who look like that every day.'

I was on a sympathetic chord here. The man practically wriggled with pleasure.

'Brother, this town is wide open. Always something hopping if you know where to look. Gals around here got too much money or too much looks, sometimes both. Feller can have himself one hell of a life if he knows what time it is.'

'Like movie people and such?' I prompted.

'Oh sure there's that crowd. Then there's all this television stuff, plus all these guys making it so fast they need help carrying it to the bank. This climate just naturally draws the broads, brother. Oh, I'm saying this town is wide open.'

'So you can't be expected to know where you met Juanita Morales?'

'Just one dame? One dame more or less out of the whole of this area, including L.A. and Hollywood? Please, brother.'

He rolled his eyes in mock despair. I grinned knowingly, the kind of grin guys like Gregg Hudson expect to get from the audience, when they talk about their qualifications for the hay-rolling championships. I didn't like him very much.

'Well, if you don't remember, I guess it doesn't matter,' I said.

'Can you try to remember something more recently? About a month ago you called the Whitton house and asked for Juanita. Can you recall why that was?'

He puckered up his mouth.

'Let's see, a month ago. Yes, I think I remember that. You're wrong about me calling her, though. I wanted to talk to Dixie about — about something else. She mentioned that the kid had walked out on her, and I asked her what happened. Yeah, I'm sure that's the way it was.'

That tallied with what Dixie Whitton had told me.

'And you haven't seen her since?'

'No. I was out to the house a coupla times while she was working there, but all I did was ask about the job, how she was doing.'

'I see. You wouldn't know of any friends she might have had, any contacts?

Somewhere I could go and ask some more questions?'

He thought about it, finally shook his head.

'Nope. Sorry. If the kid's in some kind of a jam, I'd like to help. But — '

He heaved the wide shoulders and looked at me questioningly.

It was my cue for the door.

'Well thanks for listening, anyway.'

I got up and went to the door. A small pin-up picture was stuck on the wall. Not the kind of picture for a man to be looking at too often in all this hot weather. I slipped a card halfway behind the picture.

'Telephone number's on there,' I told him. 'If you think of anything — '

'Sure, I'll call you up.'

I pulled the door behind me and went slowly back down the stairs. There was no sign of the old man as I went out into the street. As I climbed inside the car I thought I caught a quick movement at the window of apartment 8 but I couldn't be certain. I started the motor, checked the traffic and rolled away. At the right intersection I turned and pulled up around the corner. I was probably making a lot out of nothing, but Hudson had called Juanita Morales a wetback. This is an old-fashioned word, and it is used to describe Mexican illegal immigrants from the old days when they used to swim across the Rio Grande to gain access to the United States. Some people still use the word to describe them although the swimming days were mostly long past. Nowadays we had pirate air services, fast launches and the rest of the mechanised aids to modern crime. But if Hudson called her a wetback it suggested to me that he knew she hadn't any papers. And if he knew that, why should he help her in the first place, and how could he forget about it so fast in the second?

I walked back to the corner and bought a sports paper from a stand. From where I was I could easily see the front entrance to the Venice Apartments. After about five minutes a well-built man in a white sport shirt emerged. He checked the traffic both ways and crossed the street, disappearing inside the swing doors of a bar. So it was a hot afternoon and maybe Hudson could use a beer. Maybe. The place was called Mike's according to the neon sign that flickered in pointless competition with the harsh sunlight. I went over and peeked inside. It was a long room, screened booths to one side, bar occupying most of the other. I was in time to see Hudson slipping into a booth at the far end, together with a short fat man with a good humoured face. I decided I'd nothing better to do, and at least I'd get a cold glass of something. Once Hudson had sat down I went in and took the corner seat in the nearest booth, back towards Hudson. After a moment or two a tall, hefty blonde girl sauntered up and stood looking me over reflectively.

'What can I get you?'

From the tone of her voice and the little smile at the corner of her lips it was evident that not all the available service was necessarily included on the printed price list. I ogled her appreciatively.

'Well, well, what have we here? In the last eight days little lady, I have been through ten towns. If I'd seen anyone like

70

you on the trip I wouldn't have been in such a hurry.'

She was pleased.

'G'wan,' she replied. 'Ten towns, no kiddin'?'

'No kidding,' I assured her, pressing a hand over my heart.

A great revelation seemed to hit her.

'A salesman, huh?'

'Right in one, little lady. The original tired salesman, looking for a place to stop over for a day or two. Oh, don't get me wrong,' I hurried on seeing the change in expression. 'All I came in here for was a beer.'

'One beer.'

She went away to collect it from the bar. When she came back and set the beer down in front of me, she flicked half-heartedly at the table with a grubby cloth.

'What's the time, mister salesman? The clock's on the blink.'

I made a small production out of checking the time.

'Almost four.' I tapped at my wrist. 'And this little beauty hasn't put a hand out of place in eight years, Miss er — '

'Jo-Ann.' She crimped at her hair with stiff fingers. 'Eight years, huh? And not a hand out of place all that time. Bet that's more'n you can say.'

I laughed my salesman laugh.

'Say that's pretty good, pretty good, Jo-Ann. Oh, my name is Myers, Chuck Myers.'

'Pleased to meetcha,' she trilled. 'Tell you what, if you're really looking for a place to stop over, I could maybe help. I know plenty people in this town. I'll be through here at six, if you're still around.'

'I'll be around,' I winked expansively. 'Got to make one or two calls. Business, you understand. But I'll be here at six sharp, with bells on.'

Another customer signalled to her and she went away. The beer was indifferent. I lit a cigarette and sat waiting. Halfway through a second cigarette I was so lost in thought I almost missed Hudson's exit. There was a blur of someone going past and I suddenly realised it was my man. Leaving some change on the table I went out quickly, waving to Jo-Ann. Hudson headed straight across to the Venice Apartments and went inside. It seemed unlikely he would be going out again right away. If he'd got anywhere else to go he would have carried straight on from Mike's Bar. It was a reasonable assumption. I went back to the car, pulled around the corner and slid into a vacant spot by the kerb about twenty yards down from Mike's. My best bet now was the cheerful fat guy Hudson had talked to in the bar. The whole thing was ridiculous anyway. A man gets a yen for a cold drink on a hot day, so I decide to sherlock everybody he talks to. Even as I was thinking it, a maroon and cream Coastal cab suddenly swung out from the traffic stream and pulled up outside Mike's. Immediately the fat character came out, hurried across and climbed in. I let a delivery truck and a new Chevy get between us before starting after the cab. The journey wasn't far, a ten-minute run to the less fashionable end of the business section. The delivery truck was still with us and I was unsighted when the hack pulled up. One second it was two jumps ahead of me in traffic, the next it was stationary at the kerb and the fat man was riffling through some bills to pay off the driver. I pulled over fast, and the man in the Olds behind me had to brake suddenly. At such short notice he did me proud in the way of a description of my personal habits, and I couldn't blame him. I heaved out of the car and made a fast time into the twenty storey office building into which the fat man was just disappearing. There were two elevators in the lobby. I made no attempt to catch up as he stepped into the one on the right and spoke to the operator. He was the only passenger, and although I doubted whether he knew me I wasn't going to get quite that close. Not yet anyway. The red light showed at 6. I went to the other elevator.

'Six, please.'

The operator, a tired-looking middle-aged man, nodded without enthusiasm. We rode up in silence and when we reached the target area he pressed the white button and the doors slid smoothly apart.

'Six,' he said accusingly.

I nodded my thanks and stepped out. Fixed to the wall opposite was a blonde mahogany board with the sixth floor tenants printed in heavy black capitals. The fat man had disappeared. I had a choice of twelve companies. Eleven of those would be unable to help me, and I could imagine my reception at the twelfth. All I had was a description of a man, no name, and in any case the guy was probably on some entirely harmless personal business. An office door opened at the end of the passage. I swung quickly round and caught a hostile stare from a neat little dark-haired girl with a pile of papers under one arm. I pretended to be studying the list of companies again. She passed disapprovingly behind me and entered another door further along the passage. Turning, I pushed the button for the elevator the fat man had ridden in. A few seconds later the flush doors rolled back and a fair haired boy looked out at me.

'Down?' he queried.

'Just a minute.'

He looked puzzled and leaned against the door.

'What's up mister?'

'Nothing's up,' I told him. Then I held out a five-dollar bill. 'How's the think-box?'

He grinned, took the bill, sniffed at it and tucked it away in the pocket of his pants.

'Great shape,' he assured me. 'What do I have to think about?'

I lowered my voice and looked mysterious.

'This is a divorce matter,' I whispered. 'Very confidential. Catch?'

He nodded.

'And?'

'And I'm very interested in a man who just got off at this floor. Which company is he with?'

'What man, mister? We got all kinds on this floor.'

'You brought him up five minutes ago. He's medium height, fat, kind of happy looking. In a grey suit.'

The buzzer inside the elevator rang loudly.

'Oh, that one. You got a bad connection, mister. That guy don't belong here.'

'Are you sure?' I pressed.

'Sure I'm sure. Comes in quite a lot, but he don't belong to us.'

I looked disappointed.

'That's bad,' I sighed. 'Still I ought to follow it through, I guess. My information ain't what it used to be. Where does the tub go?'

The elevator boy jerked his thumb to the right.

'Calls in on the tourist agency. Say, you think maybe one of the girls in there — ?'

I wagged my head sideways. The buzzer was working overtime now.

'No. This is nothing like that. Some very important people mixed up in this enquiry. Still, thanks for the help. Like you said, I got a bad connection.'

He looked worried.

'Say, how about the fin?'

'That's O.K.,' I told him. 'You held up your end. Not your fault I had it wrong.'

'Well, thanks,' he grinned. Then he made a face at the insistent buzzer. 'Say, if you don't mind I'd better go answer that customer.'

'Sure. Thanks, anyway.'

The doors closed and he was gone. I checked the company names again. There it was, the M. City Tourist Agency, F7. I walked along till I came to 7. The glass-panelled door carried only the name of the company and the word 'Enquiries'. I didn't want to go in while the fat man was there. The outfit next door was the Exmoor Novelty Co. I lounged around outside waiting. It seemed a long while before the door of the M. City Tourist Agency began to open inwards. Immediately I turned my back and opened the door of the Exmoor Novelty Co. The fat man came out and bustled up the corridor. I wondered if he was always in a hurry like that. Just a naturally breathless character. I was now half way inside the door. A little man peered anxiously over the top of a desk.

'Yes?'

I looked around, puzzled. Then it dawned on me.

'Oh say, I'm sorry. Wrong door.'

'Quite all right.'

I backed out again, and walked along to the M. City Tourist Agency. I didn't expect what I saw. There were two desks in the small room. All the fittings on each were identical. Behind them sat two of the most beautiful girls I'd ever seen. One was a shimmering silver blonde, in a black linen dress severely cut, and open at the throat. The other had shining coal-black hair. Her dress was white linen, and exactly the same style as her room-mate's. They both smiled. It was like being caught in the crossfire between opposing battle-wagons.

'Good afternoon,' said the blonde.

'Could we help you?' said the brunette.

I closed the door. There was a counter with a flap at the side. I leaned on it and looked at each in turn.

'Funny thing,' I confessed. 'When I came in here, I knew why. Now something's driven it clean out of my head.'

They smiled again. It was very relaxing. The M. City Tourist Agency knew its business. A harmless male could easily go in to make an enquiry about connections to San Francisco, and come out fully booked for a round-world cruise. To the right was a gold painted door with one word on it, 'Manager'. I nodded towards it.

'I want to see your boss. Police matter.'

The smiles and all attached radiance were switched off as though there'd been a power failure. The blonde said,

'I'm not sure whether Mr. Hartley is here — '

'He's here,' I interrupted. 'Now you tell him I'm here. The name is Preston.'

She glanced at the other girl, who shrugged her beautiful shoulders.

'Don't let's delay the course of justice,' she observed.

The blonde then got up and crossed to the gold door. The journey only lasted a few feet, but this one managed to put plenty of production into it. The dark one made no pretence of taking any further interest in me. She picked up a pencil and began flicking through a brightly coloured folder, making an occasional note on the lemon-coloured pad at her side. Soon the blonde reappeared, leaving the manager's door partly open.

'Mr. Hartley will see you now.'

I eased up the counter-flap, stepped through and smiled my thanks.

She ignored me altogether and went back to her desk. I pushed the gold door wide and took a look at Mr. Hartley. He was a smooth one. White linen suit, heavy blue silk tie, neat pocket handkerchief. Not too much handkerchief. Early forties, slim, good-looking without any noticeable strength about the jaws and chin. He had eyes of pale blue and a young executive haircut. On the rosewood desk stood an ivory strip with the legend 'Myron C. Hartley'. Myron C. Hartley, you were entitled to assume, was going places.

He flashed me a wide, engaging smile. I was not engaged.

'Well, Mr. Preston, isn't it? What can I do for the police?'

He didn't offer to shake hands, which was a relief.

'I wouldn't know,' I replied. 'I'm not a policeman.'

He looked confused.

'But I don't understand. My assistant distinctly told me — '

'She told you it was a police matter. It is. That doesn't make me a policeman. Any more than it makes you a suspect — or have I said the wrong thing?'

He looked at me coolly. One thing a white linen suit does for the right man. Certainly makes him look cool.

'Having got into my office under false pretences,' he said in level tones, 'Would you say what you have to say and leave. I have work to do.'

'Sure.'

I went over for a closer look at a poster for Catalina. There was a girl lying on one of those inflated beach-couch things.

'I've been to Catalina a few times,' I told him. 'Never yet seen anything like that.'

'No doubt. You would hardly expect to find girls of that quality in the cheaper hotels. I can give you one more minute precisely.'

He consulted the thick gold watch strapped round his slender wrist.

'Might be enough,' I conceded.

'Where's Juanita Morales?'

Now he looked puzzled.

'Juanita Morales? Who would she be?'

I walked over to the desk, leaned on it and stuck my face close to Hartley's.

'It's been a hot day. A long day. Don't waste my time. Where is she?'

He looked straight into my eyes.

'I don't know who you are or what you're talking about. Now please go away, before I summon the security people here.'

I leaned back and straightened up.

'Who I am is Preston.' I dropped a card in front of him. He made no move either to pick it up or look at it. 'What I am and where you find me is on the card. I want Juanita Morales. I haven't been to the cops yet with what I've got. You could say I'm waiting to see if I hear a better offer. But I won't wait after tonight. Tomorrow morning I'll be at police headquarters, singing like a little canary bird.'

He shook his head in amusement.

'You're a strange man. You barge in here for the sole purpose of talking nonsense. I still don't know what this is all about.'

'O.K. I'll take my rubbish to the law-boys in the morning. Maybe they'll be able to follow me a little better.'

I left him sitting quite still with that infuriating little smile of tolerant amusement on his face. My unread card lay in front of him. Outside, the Dolly sisters let me stare at the tops of their bent heads. It was a pity to get in dutch with two such dames all in one afternoon. Especially since I was undoubtedly wasting everybody's time.

I didn't see the friendly elevator man in the lobby. Outside, I got into the car and headed for the office. It was already five fifteen.

4

Florence Digby was closing up the store when I arrived. Her desk was mathematically tidy, and she was just locking up the file cabinets.

'I was about to leave,' she said unnecessarily. 'Was there anything for me before I go?'

'No thanks, you go along. I'll be here a while. May get a break on the Morales girl.'

She nodded. I went in to my own office and looked up Mike's Bar in the telephone directory. Then I called the number. A man answered.

'Like to talk to Jo-Ann,' I told him.

'Who is this?'

'Myers. Tell her it's Chuck Myers.'

'O.K. She's serving a customer. May take a coupla minutes.'

He put the receiver down on some hard surface and I rubbed my ear where the explosion went off. After a while Jo-Ann came on. She didn't sound too friendly.

'A brush, huh?'

'Now wait a minute, honey, calm down. Look, you think I went to all that trouble to get a date with you, just so I could wriggle out of it two hours later?'

She seemed slightly mollified.

'Well, I don't know. Nothing any man does surprises me any more.'

'Another thing,' I insisted. 'If I didn't want to see you I'd just forget to turn up, right?'

'Right, I guess. Well, what's the story?'

'One of my contacts has me all set to meet somebody tonight. Could be a big thing. Could increase my commission by about thirty bucks a week. I can't afford to lose that kind of money.'

'I guess not. So what happens?'

'I'm due in Fresno tomorrow night, so it looks like no deal this week anyhow. But I'll be back this way in two weeks time. How about if I call in for a glass of beer then?'

I didn't want to lose touch with Jo-Ann altogether. She might still be useful some time. She seemed to swallow the story anyway.

'O.K. I suppose you gotta think about your business. If I'm still here when you drop by maybe we can try again.'

I told her I certainly hoped so, and she told me she certainly hoped so too and I broke the connection. Florence Digby stuck her head round the door.

'Shall I lock the office up, when I leave?'

'No thanks. I'm hoping for a visitor.'

'All right. Goodnight, Mr. Preston.'

'Goodnight, Miss Digby.'

I made myself as comfortable as possible and settled down to wait. When I fixed the date with Jo-Ann I'd been following the old rule of not ignoring any possibility. That was before I was led to the M. City Tourist Agency. Jo-Ann may or may not be in possession of some small piece of information that could help me. If there was any connection between my business and the hurried visit of the little fat man to the agency, the manager, Hartley, would certainly know a lot more. I'd been poking around here and there, telling everybody what I was after, and I'd rounded off the day by threatening

Hartley with the law. Now seemed like the time to sit and wait. Not much use expecting anyone to contact me if I was wandering all over town.

By seven-thirty I was beginning to wonder whether I had such a good idea when I heard the door of the outer office. Not knowing what to expect I got ready for any kind of visitor. Then, to my surprise, there was a knock at my door.

'Come in.'

It opened, and two men came in. Whatever I'd been expecting, it certainly wasn't these two. They were both in their early twenties, scrubbed clean and glowing with health. Unmistakable college graduates, just started in advertising or whatever. The taller had red hair, the other boy was fair, otherwise I couldn't put a pin between them.

'Mark Preston?' enquired the redhead. I called him One.

'That's me. What can I do for you?'

'May we come in for a minute?'

This was from the fair one, Two.

'Why not?'

They came into the room, Two closing

the door. They found chairs, parked. I waited.

'All right, you're in. What is it, tickets for a graduation ball?'

One smiled. So did Two. He said

'No, Mr. Preston. We've come about a little matter you've been taking an interest in.'

'Really? I have lots of interests. Incidentally, I usually like to know who I'm talking to.'

'That won't be necessary in this case,' said One. 'You see, we've only come here as a favour to a friend. Naturally we don't wish to be involved personally.'

'How about the friend?' I countered. 'Does he have a name?'

Two smiled again, and shook his head.

'Sorry. This is all rather delicate. We've come to talk about a young lady. A Miss Morales.'

Nothing surprises me any more. I lit a cigarette and sat back.

'All right, go ahead. Talk about her.'

One coughed, then fidgetted with his tie before he spoke.

'Why are you interested in Miss

Morales, Mr. Preston?'

I laughed. I couldn't help it.

'Look, boys, this isn't going to do, at all. I didn't come to you, you came to me. This is my office, remember? Now, if you've got something to tell me about Miss Morales, O.K. I'm listening. But if you just came here to peek at my cards it's no deal.'

They looked at each other anxiously. Finally One nodded. Two said, 'May we have your word that nothing of what we tell you will go outside these four walls?'

'No,' I said emphatically. 'I don't want to know for my own amusement. There's someone else who's interested.'

'Ah. Well, let me put it this way,' said One. 'If you learned something about the young lady that wasn't to her credit, would you be surprised?'

'Not very.'

'And if there was someone else involved with her, someone who was nothing to do with you at all, would you be prepared not to pursue the identity of that other person?'

I thought about that.

'That's a rough one,' I admitted. 'You mean if the girl and your friend committed a murder, will I keep the friend out of it? Hardly.'

One smiled very pleasantly and shook his head.

'It isn't anything like that. There is nothing criminal involved here. The offence is — er — social.'

'Suppose you tell me what it is?' I said pointedly.

'Very well,' One hitched nervously at the right leg of his pants. 'Miss Morales is pregnant. The man responsible is a mutual friend of this gentleman's and mine.'

And that was about what I'd expected. I tried to look shocked.

'Pregnant? Well, that's a very serious matter. What does this friend of yours propose to do about it?'

Two came in again, eagerly.

'He is behaving as a gentleman should I assure you. He's standing by the girl, paying all her bills, everything.'

'Uh huh. Is he going to marry her?'

They both looked sheepish.

'Well,' said Two. 'No, he can scarcely be expected to do that. It would ruin him. But you can have our assurance — '

'I already have,' I reminded him. 'I shall need a little more than that. Where's the girl?'

'We thought you'd probably wish to talk with her. A meeting has been arranged. Could you come with us now?'

'Where to?'

'A hotel in town. We've rented a suite for Miss Morales for the evening.'

'Before we go, how'd you boys know I was asking about her?'

They were both standing now.

'Does it matter?' queried One.

'It could. I told some weird people. People who shouldn't know guys like you two.'

Two smiled again.

'It was our friend who contacted us, and asked us to see you.'

'And he still doesn't have a name,' I made it a statement.

'Sorry.'

★ ★ ★

The Hotel Miami is a large, plushy affair dominating Whitton Avenue. The college boys had a cab waiting outside my office, and we all rode together. Neither of them mentioned where we were going until the jockey braked outside the main entrance to the hotel.

'We're here,' announced One.

I followed him through the glass swing doors into the air-conditioned foyer. We went up to the desk, and One addressed the clerk.

'Miss Morales' suite, please.'

'The lady is expecting you?' enquired the clerk.

'Yes. Tell her it's Mr. Preston and his party.'

While the clerk spoke into the desk telephone I admired the way in which One had avoided letting me know his name. The clerk was soon finished.

'Thank you, gentlemen. Suite 107, third floor.'

We moved off to the bank of elevators and rode up to three. Then we all marched down the wide hallway looking for 107. When we found it One pressed the buzzer, then opened the door. We went in. A girl was standing by the windows, looking at us. She was raven-haired, young and probably beautiful when she didn't look so ill. From the waist down she was shapeless in voluminous light-weight coat.

'Juanita, this is Mr. Preston, whom we told you about,' said One.

'Señor Preston,' she inclined her head in acknowledgement. 'According to my friends you wish to see me. What about?'

The voice was not unmusical and certainly had nothing of the peon in it. Father Tomaso and the mission school had done their work well.

'How do you do, Miss Morales. Yes, I've been trying to find you. Would it be possible for us to talk alone?'

I half-expected an argument from the All-Americans, but Two said immediately.

'Certainly. Talk as much as you want. We'll wait downstairs in the bar. If you want to see us later, Preston, that's where we'll be. If not, we'll say goodnight now.'

I nodded as the two of them left. I was hoping their departure might bring about some change in Juanita's attitude, which was cool. It remained cool.

'Very well, señor, we are alone. Please come to the point.'

She walked slowly and awkwardly to a high-backed chair and sat down. I found myself a seat, too.

'Mind if I smoke?'

She watched impassively while I stuck an Old Favourite in my face and flicked my lighter.

'Your family hired me to find you, Juanita,' I told her.

She caught her breath sharply.

'My family? But this cannot be. They are far from here.'

'Not so far.' I said gently. 'Not so far when a daughter runs away from home, writes a few letters and then disappears. They retained me to find you, and here I am. The question is, what do we do now?'

Her face was troubled.

'I do not understand at all. My people are very poor, it costs much money to employ a man like you.'

'Your father will work for years to pay it back,' I admitted. 'Why don't you tell me what happened.'

'What happened? Hah,' she said scornfully. 'Can't you see what happened señor? Can't you see what always happens when the little country girl comes to the big city?'

'I see a young girl who's going to have a baby in a strange town where she probably hasn't any friends. Who's the man?'

She shook her head swiftly.

'I am very fortunate, señor. Most girls in my position have to suffer alone. But I am fortunate. This man, he blames himself as much as me — '

'Which is considerate of him,' I butted in.

'Oh it is easy to make judgment from outside, señor. But most men would have turned their backs. This one has accepted his responsibility. He will stand by me until — until my bad time is over.'

'I see. And then?'

'Quien sabe? It does not matter. This is the time that matters. He has promised to do everything in his power to help me, and in return I must keep his name out of it. It is more than fair.'

Put like that, I had to admit the guy had something. Nine out of ten would have been on the next train out.

'What am I to tell your father?'

'My father? You have seen him?'

'Yes. He is very well. Why did you stop writing home?'

She unclasped her hands expressively.

'I don't know. It was foolish. When I ran away from Mrs. Whitton I was so frightened. So afraid, I just hoped to die. I had so much fear my poor family would get to know of this thing. It seemed to me if I stopped telling anyone where I was, it would be as though I ceased to exist. Anyway I did not believe anything like this could really be happening to me. Soon I would realise it was all a dream, then I could go home, and everything would be just like always again.' She smiled sadly. 'We think foolish things when we are very afraid, señor.'

'And now? Now that you see things differently, why not write?'

She nodded.

'I have been so absorbed with my own affairs I have not given thought to others. I will write to them tomorrow.'

'Your father is right here in this city,' I informed her. 'I could have you with him in twenty minutes.'

A joyous look came on her face.

'He is here?' Then the look disappeared. 'No, it is no use. I cannot see my father. He must never know of this.'

She patted at her middle.

'Then what must I tell him?' I pressed.

'Tell him anything. Tell him you met a friend, someone who knows me. I am away in — in — Nevada at the moment, but I am going to write to him when I return.'

I thought about that.

'How would this friend know you were going to write, when it's been so long since your last letter?'

Her brows crinkled in concentration.

'Because I had an accident. That's it, an accident. I went to Sun Valley for a ski-ing vacation and broke my writing arm in several places.'

'Sounds all right.'

I got up and searched around for a card.

'There's my address and telephone number. I know you're being looked after by this man whoever he is, but if you need anything, anything at all, let me know. Will you do that?'

She nodded.

'I will. I am most grateful, Señor Preston. People have been — so kind.'

Her voice started to choke up, the tears were not far away. I felt like hell, but there was nothing I could do. What had happened to Juanita Morales was happening every day of the week. Only most of the guys forget to stick around and pick up the check. I wished her good luck and left. On the way down in the elevator I was rehearsing my part in the interview I would have to have with Ramon Morales. I wasn't looking forward to it a bit. A man who hitches three hundred miles has a right to expect something better than a pack of lies when he gets the other end. The only consolation was, the truth would certainly not be as good as the fiction. Not to his ears, anyway.

I didn't look in the bar. There was nothing I had to say to the college boys. On the way I had a hunch and stopped by the desk.

'Good evening, sir.' It was the same clerk.

'We already met,' I reminded him. 'I called on Miss Morales just a few minutes ago, remember?'

He inspected me with care.

'I do, sir. Suite 107 wasn't it?'

'It was. There were two other men with me.'

'Really, sir.'

'Really.' I described One and Two. 'Is it coming back?'

'Yes, indeed it is. Yes I remember it all quite distinctly.'

He seemed quite excited about it. I was glad I wasn't going to ask about something in the dim past, like about noon on the same day.

'Now those two young men, do you happen to know who they are?'

He brightened even further.

'Why yes, I do. Not their names of

course but I've seen them in the hotel several times in the past few months. Friends, or rather, business associates of Mr. Hartley, you know.'

It was just like Christmas.

'Mr. Hartley? I'm afraid I don't know him,' I was puzzled.

'Then, sir, you are certainly not in the hotel business. Not in Monkton City anyway. Mr. Hartley books in the conventions, or most of them.'

'I see. And those two work for him.'

'So far as one can tell, sir, yes. You know Mr. Hartley always creates such an atmosphere when he's handling a convention. Everyone is so friendly and pleasant, it's often hard to know which people are taking part and which are running the organising side.'

'Sounds like a nice guy,' I remarked.

I made it Christmas for the clerk, too. I left two fives on the counter.

'It's Christmas,' I told him. He didn't get it.

5

I caught a cab back to my apartment at Parkside Towers. The Towers are very much on the right side of town, and the rental, accordingly, is very much on the wrong side of exorbitant. Part of the price is attributed to the calm and peaceful surroundings. I didn't think these were at all improved by the plain police sedan which crouched at the kerb a few yards up from where I paid off the cab-driver. When I let myself in to the apartment I found out why the sedan was there. A man was sprawled deeply in one of my best chairs. A man whose broad shoulders and barrel chest made the chair look like a child's model.

'Thought I'd come inside and wait,' was his greeting. 'Didn't figure you'd mind, huh, Preston?'

'You know me, Randall,' I replied. 'Anything for our brave boys in blue.'

It wasn't strictly accurate. Gil Randall

is a sergeant in the Homicide Detail, which is a plain-clothes assignment. I wasn't too pleased to see him. The trouble with Randall, he's built like an ox, with a thick peasant face that has one of two effects on people. They either think the man is half-asleep, or else that he's a prime example of arrested mental development. Either way they lose. If Randall ever does sleep, I've never heard about it, and as far as his mental development is concerned you could get a dozen testimonials from any jail in the state. If Randall was on the prowl it always meant big trouble, and that was something I wanted to stay away from.

'What's this all about?' I asked him.

He sat up a little straighter in the chair and looked me over.

'Missed you, Preston. Haven't seen you in months. Just thought I'd drop over for a little chat. You know.'

'Sure, I know. The last little chat we had lasted about six hours. The inside of my head was like a rubber jelly for days.'

'Ah,' he shrugged. 'That was business. Man has to make a living. This is more social. Yeah, that's it. A social call.'

'Then you won't mind if I have a drink.'

I went over to the small table where I keep a supply, and poured myself a middle-sized scotch. Then I sat down facing my visitor.

'I didn't offer you one because I've never known you accept before,' I explained. 'Well O.K. I'm ready. Get social.'

His eyes narrowed very slightly, but he laughed.

'Well, how've you been? Or shall I say, where?'

'Tonight?' I queried.

'Tonight, today, I'm interested.'

'Does Rourke know you're interested?'

'The lieutenant and I are very old friends,' he said gently. 'He knows I'm interested. I'll come clean with you, Preston. He's interested, too. Where were you?'

I swallowed some of the drink. It was good.

'Well now, let's see. I got up early — '

I went into a long explanation about

what I had for breakfast. When I was fully into my stride Randall interrupted.

'All right, it's your round. We'll probably get on a little quicker if I just ask a few harmless questions.'

'We'd get on a little better if I knew what this was all about,' I told him.

'You don't know? Ever hear of a man named Gregg Hudson?'

'Hudson?' I looked like a man trying to remember whether he ever heard of a man named Gregg Hudson.

'Yes, Hudson. H-U-D-S-O-N. Like the river.'

'It does sound familiar,' I admitted. 'Damned if I can place him though, right this minute.'

'You know, Preston, you're slowing up. If this goes on you'll have to find some other kind of work. This man you don't remember, you were talking with him this afternoon.'

'I was?'

'At about three o'clock, give or take a few minutes. The janitor remembers you. Besides, you left your business card in the guy's room.'

'Look, Sergeant, let me in on this will you? What makes it important whether I know Hudson or not? And why don't you ask him about it?'

He shifted in the chair and scowled.

'Hudson ain't making a lotta sense right now. Could be something to do with the ice-pick that's sticking in his back.'

I'd been half-expecting to hear something of the kind. The Monkton City Police Department doesn't send Gil Randall out on parking beefs.

'I see.'

It wasn't a very bright remark but it was the best I could do at the moment. If I'd had some reason to expect a development of the kind I could have had a whole bookful of interesting dialogue, most of it designed to keep the law off my back while I got on with my own affairs. But this was the curved ball. Here was a straightforward case of a missing girl who got herself in trouble. I'd had the breaks, found the girl, straightened the whole thing out in a matter of hours. Now Hudson had to get himself killed. My own interest in him was over, and all that stood to happen to me now was a revoked licence and a jail sentence for aiding illegal immigrants. It was very bad luck indeed.

'You don't seem very surprised,' observed Randall.

'Surprised? Well I'm surprised, naturally. In an offhand way. I'm not any more surprised than I would be if it were anybody else in town. As I told you I don't know the man.'

'But you were there this afternoon,' insisted the detective.

'O.K., so I was there this afternoon. I talked with him for five minutes or so. Never seen him before or since. I can't help you.'

Randall waved a reproving finger about the size of a baseball bat.

'Modesty is a very becoming thing, but you're pushing it, Preston. Who says you can't help me? Let's bat it around. Like for instance, what did you talk to Hudson about?'

'Will it do any good, if I just tell you I made a routine call in connection with something I'm working on? It didn't have anything to do with ice-picks or murder.'

Slowly, he shook his head.

'No it won't do a damned bit of good.'

'All right. I called on Hudson on a routine matter. Routine but confidential. The law says I don't have to divulge the nature of my business, or the name of my client, without that client's permission.'

'Don't tell me what the law says,' he replied irritably. 'The law is my business. There's another bit of law you may have heard of. Something about obstructing the course of justice by withholding information.'

'Not quite right. Information of a material nature is the exact wording I think.'

Randall never blusters when he's annoyed. He gets calm, icy calm. And it usually bodes no good for somebody. Somebody like me.

'When I came in here I wasn't expecting any trouble. Seems I'm getting it. Now you just 'phone your confidential client and ask if it's O.K. to spill. Otherwise I'm going to think you're being hard to get on with. I mean it, Preston.'

Inside I was cursing. Cursing the miserable luck that sent me a client like Ramon Estaban Morales on the very day a chaser like Hudson got himself bumped off. For a hundred dollars I had the choice. I could either toss overboard the relationship with the police which had taken me years to build up, or I could go to jail. Fine. While I was busy thinking what to do the telephone shrilled suddenly. Randall shifted so he could watch me as I picked it up.

'Preston.'

There was a sigh at the other end then a woman's voice, deep.

'Lover man, thought you were going to call me?'

It was Dixie Whitton, and whatever the name of that stuff was she'd been drinking when I last saw her, it was beginning to slur her voice.

'Why, good evening, Mrs. Whitton.'

I took a peek at Randall's face to see if the name registered. By this time I should know better. Randall's face never gives away a thing. Turning my back on him, I made a show of dropping my voice and seeming ill-at-ease. Just the same I made sure my new confidential tone was clearly audible to the man from Homicide.

'Now all of a sudden I'm Mrs. Whitton?' she queried. 'You either have a bad memory, or a stack of numbers in your book, brother. What became of that melody you were working on this morning?'

'Yes, I'm sorry, Mrs. Whitton, I should have called sooner. I'm afraid I can't discuss it at the moment. There's someone with me. A police officer.'

'Oh,' she laughed lazily, 'I get it. Putting on an act for the police. What's the trouble, Preston? Some poor girl, sworn out a complaint because you didn't call her?'

'No,' I said urgently, 'I assure you it has nothing to do with our business. Perhaps I could call you later. Are you at home?'

'At this hour? You must be crazy. No, it's a Circle number. Wait a minute — Here. Double-o, 5-2-9-1. Got it?'

'I have it, Mrs. Whitton. I'll call as soon as possible.'

'See you do.'

She hung up. I resisted an impulse to do a dance round the apartment and turned back to Randall. He regarded me without affection.

'Mrs. Whitton? She's your client?'

'I didn't say that, Randall,' I said cagily.

'I've got ears,' he snorted. 'Which one is it, the old lady or one of the wives?'

I tried to look wise, and made no reply. Randall rose, a mountain of a man emerging from the depths of the chair. A displeased mountain.

'Disappointed in you. Thought I could rely on you for a little co-operation.'

'Sorry, Randall. It's out of my hands.'

'It's not out of mine. Oh, I know you can hide behind the Whitton name for a while. More than my shield is worth to make myself a nuisance with that family. But there'll be other capers, other times. Around me, watch yourself.'

He left. I don't usually reckon to win any popularity contests with the Department, but just the same it was a pity for Randall to go sour on me. Not that I blamed him. My immediate problem was what to do about Dixie Whitton. I had a

111

feeling she hadn't called merely to ask how I was. I also knew I could buy a lot of trouble around a woman like that. One thing was certain, I'd have to call her. I'd need to keep in some kind of contact with the girl if I wanted the Homicide boys to go on thinking she was my client. I got through to the Circle number. As the receiver was lifted at the other end I got a background of bar noises.

'Hallo.'

A man's voice, cool and impersonal.

'I want to speak with Mrs. Whitton, please.'

'Who is this?'

'Just say it's a man who wants to speak to Mrs. Whitton.'

'Hold on.'

While I waited I could hear the hum of conversation in a busy room. An occasional laugh and the tinkle of glasses. She was probably in some bar. Soon she spoke.

'I'm Mrs. Whitton,' she said. 'Are you the man?'

'It's early to tell yet,' I replied. 'We only met this morning.'

'Oh, that man. You know the Oyster's Cloister?'

'I've been there.'

'That's where I am, lover. Just get here before I die of boredom.'

'Are you alone?' I asked.

'What would I be doing in a place like this alone? No, I have one or two people with me. But no man with me, not in that sense, if that's what you mean.'

'That's what I mean. I'll be there in fifteen minutes.'

Some guys never know when they've got enough trouble. Dixie Whitton was no ordinary dame. First she was married, and I have a rule about that. Second, her husband and his family practically owned the town. On top of all that, Dixie herself was a wild and unpredictable person. I might have to do some very fancy balancing before the night was through.

★ ★ ★

The Oyster's Cloister was one of the spots on the popular list at present. It had been running for years without any spectacular success, but all of a sudden it was the place to go, so the night-lifers were giving it a play. The Cloister was owned by Reuben Krantz, an old friend of mine. Tonight he was talking to some people in the entrance as I arrived. When he saw me he smiled and excused himself.

'Well, Preston. Nice to see you. You haven't been around in a while.'

We shook hands.

'Hallo, Krantz. Didn't think you'd want my kind of business with all these names crowding the bar.'

He snorted and lowered his voice.

'These crums. Them I can do without. So they spend their money. Some of the behaviour I've had to put up with from this crowd you wouldn't believe.'

I grinned, and ran an appreciative finger down the lapel of his immaculate jacket.

'Still, it does keep a few rags on a man's back.'

'You got me. Come and have a drink.'

He turned to lead me inside but I held him back.

'Sorry, I have to meet somebody here. Maybe later.'

'O.K.'

I nodded and went on in. The place was busy, and I could spot half a dozen headline names in the first minute. Dixie Whitton was with two men and another woman at a side table. She was engaged in animated conversation and didn't even look up when I stood beside her.

'Isn't this our dance, Mrs. Whitton?' I said.

She looked up then. So did the others. I thought the youngish man with the fair moustache looked briefly annoyed.

'Ah here you are at last. Come and sit next to me.' Turning to the dreamy-eyed silver blonde girl, she said, 'Isn't he gorgeous?'

'He's beautiful,' murmured the blonde. She hardly looked in my direction.

'So you're one of these fabulous private eyes,' said Moustache.

'Quite a life you guys lead.'

There was an inflexion to his tone that told me it wouldn't break his heart if I wanted to make something out of any of his remarks. He probably had plans of his own for Dixie Whitton.

'It isn't always the way they play it up in the papers,' I told him evenly. 'Most of the time it's like any other job. What line are you in?'

'Me? Why, I'm in the meat trade.'

'With what I'm paying for steaks you ought to be able to live quite a life yourself,' I remarked.

They all laughed. It wasn't funny enough to rate a laugh. A polite smile should have been the top reaction.

'Oh, lover, you don't get it at all.' Dixie turned to me and slipped her arm through mine. 'Harry doesn't mean that kind of meat. Talent on the hoof, that's Harry's line. You know 'Fifty Gorgeous Girls — Count 'Em'. He finds the girls. Harry Swenson. You must have heard of him.'

The others were watching me with amusement.

'Sure, I've heard of you,' I admitted. I hadn't, but there was no need to make a production out of it.

The other man then started to tell

some long story about a bunch of people I'd never heard of, but which had the others rolling in the aisles. I was beginning to wonder exactly what I was doing there, when Dixie suddenly announced

'We're leaving. Sorry to break up the party but my very private detective wants to ask me lots of lovely questions. Don't you, man?'

'One or two come to mind,' I replied.

As we stood up, Swenson said in a surprised voice.

'Two? What's the other one, Preston?'

I looked at Dixie's dress. Vivid scarlet, it had no back at all, and in front was cut so low it seemed on the verge of falling off at any second.

'I'm going to ask her where she hid the body.'

While she went to tidy herself I leaned at the end of the bar. I could see the table we'd just left. The other man, whose name I never did find out, had launched out on another one of his tales. A new arrival, a man, stood a few feet away from me searching the crowd. I didn't bother to look at him till I saw he was making for

Swenson and the others. They all greeted him, and he sat down half-facing in my direction. I saw his face clearly then. It was Myron C. Hartley, the manager of the M. City Tourist Agency, and he looked like hell. I didn't have much time to think about that because Dixie Whitton appeared suddenly at my elbow.

'Let's get out of this and talk about those questions,' she said.

6

We didn't talk as I drove out of town. Dixie relaxed on the seat beside me, resting her shining black hair on the back and staring up at the indigo sky. The moon was in the third quarter, and hung there smiling down at all the guys who were lucky enough to be abroad with a beautiful woman on a night that was made for beautiful women. A few miles out I turned off on to the beach and pulled up. We sat facing out across the Pacific which rolled to a lazy halt about twenty feet away. Dixie stirred, as though just realising we'd stopped moving.

'H'm,' she stretched luxuriously. 'Question time?'

'If you're ready,' I told her, passing over a cigarette.

'I like the interrogation room,' she murmured, turning towards me. 'I'm ready.'

I snapped my lighter between us. That wasn't at all what was expected. She looked at the flame in some surprise, shrugged, then leaned forward to light her cigarette.

'It'll take me ten minutes to smoke this,' she informed me. 'You must have an awful lot of questions.'

'A few,' I admitted. 'Like what happened after I left you this morning?'

'Huh? Happened? Nothing happened. I don't get it.'

I turned my head so I could look into her face.

'Private detectives don't drop around every day I imagine. Did you happen to mention me to anybody?'

'No. Should I have?'

'I'll start again. You told me a man named Gregg Hudson brought the Morales girl to work for you.'

'That's right. You can ask him,' she said in a puzzled tone.

'I already asked him. He told me he knew nothing about her. Then I dug around a little bit and finally found the girl.'

For the first time she showed some interest.

'You did? Well that's pretty fast work. What was the big mystery? Did you find out why she walked out on me?'

'She told me to take a running kick at my head. In Spanish.'

Dixie chuckled.

'Never mind, lover. All part of the scene. Only you get a big consolation prize. Through looking for her, you met me. May turn out to be quite a day in your life.'

'It already has. Through looking for Juanita I also met Gregg Hudson. It was quite a day in his life, too. The last one.'

She looked at me queerly.

'I don't get that. What does it mean?'

'It means he's dead, angel.'

She shook her head, slowly.

'I don't believe it.'

'Believe what you like. There's a corpse professing to be Hudson on refrigerated shelf nine at the city morgue.'

She drew away from me into the far corner as if trying to get as much distance between us as possible.

'But how did he die?'

'Somebody left an ice pick in his back.'

I tried to blow a smoke ring up into the night, but the breeze from the ocean was too strong. Dixie was huddled up with her own thoughts.

'Who did it?' she asked, in a lifeless tone.

'According to the police, I'm as good a suspect as anybody. They don't really think I did it, but they know I was there this afternoon.'

'But you didn't even know the man.' She was talking half to herself.

'Correct,' I confirmed. 'But you did. You told me there was a man named Gregg Hudson. I went to see him. Soon after, he's dead. Could it be anything to do with my visit?'

'How could it have been? You found Juanita Morales, you say. So it's not a case of anybody killing Gregg to prevent you from tracing the girl, is it? And she was your only connection with him.'

'But not yours,' I said softly.

'You're going too fast for me again.'

'Hudson was a big ladies man. You told

me so, he told me so. That makes it unanimous. When you spoke about him your voice wasn't altogether dripping with loving kindness.'

'Why should it? I didn't like him too well. Hey,' the voice became sharper, 'you're not suggesting I had anything to do with — ? Ah, that's crazy.'

'Why? Somebody killed him. When these Casanovas get bumped off, it's always by some rejected woman, or the husband of one who hasn't been rejected yet.'

She laughed slightly. There was more contempt than humour in the sound.

'Husband? You mean Floyd? Brother, you really don't know much about my husband if you think he'd kill anybody over me. Why, he wouldn't walk across the street to stop me doing a strip for a bunch of drunken sailors in broad daylight.'

'Like that?'

I looked at her as she sat staring through the wind-shield. There was a curious expression on her face, one I couldn't fathom. Maybe if Floyd Whitton

Junior had a different attitude towards his wife he'd have a different wife. Anyway, it was none of my business.

'Tell me about Hudson.'

It seemed a good idea to avoid involvement with the Whitton family troubles. Dixie pulled herself away from those private thoughts.

'Gregg? Not much to tell. He was big, good-looking, nice when it suited him. Woman crazy. He always says — said — he'd wind up the champion of the whole Pacific coast for sleeping around.'

There was an edged sneer in her voice.

'He's getting a good long sleep now,' I reminded her. 'The point is, who arranged it? Did he do work of any kind? Any business connections?'

She shrugged.

'If he did, he never spoke of it. He was a glad hander, a back-slapping character. Know what he always reminded me of?'

'Uh uh,' I negatived.

'When he was in one of these good-guy, college-kid moods, I always used to think of those creeps who emcee at talent contests. You know, the corny gags and the phoney goodwill?'

'I know. I only saw him for a few minutes but I know what you mean.'

'Look, are we nearly through with the questions now? I'm getting cold.'

Whatever thoughts might have been in Dixie Whitton's mind when she left the Oyster's Cloister with me, they were long gone. All the atmosphere of warm intimacy which she could generate like a powerhouse was now dispersed. The news about Hudson's murder had been like the throwing of a switch. To the 'off' position. In one way it was quite a relief. My problem of how to avoid getting too involved with the wife of one of the town's top citizens was neatly resolved. The journey back into town was as silent as the trip out, but it was a different kind of silence. Now she was just a girl in a car being driven somewhere by somebody. Anybody. I was anybody, and I preferred it. As we entered the outskirts of Monkton she said,

'Take me back to the Cloister, please. Maybe my friends will still be there.'

The word 'friends' had a special

inflexion which left me out of the definition. When I drew in to the kerb outside Krantz's place, I waved away the uniformed doorman who came from the shadows.

'Look will you do something for me?' I asked Dixie.

'It depends.'

All she wanted was to get away from me, get away from talk about death and policemen. To get into the bright interior of the bar where those things would soon lose their reality.

'If you think of anything about Hudson, or just anything that might help clear this up, will you call me?'

She nodded briefly.

'I promise you one thing. If I call you it'll be for that reason. Frankly, Preston, you're just a little bit disappointing in other directions. You have an untaking line in conversation.'

She stepped out on to the sidewalk and moved into the lighted rectangle that was the entrance to the Oyster's Cloister. I waited a couple of minutes then climbed out of the car and walked over to where

126

the doorman stood. I held out a dollar bill.

'Ask Mr. Krantz if he can spare me a minute, will you?'

He took the bill, eyed me carefully and said,

'He's only just inside the bar.'

'Sure, but there's someone in there I don't want to see me. A lady. You know how it is.'

'Who shall I say wants him?'

'Just tell him he owes me a drink.'

He had another look at me, shrugged and went inside. He was soon back, Krantz a foot behind him.

'This is the man, Mr. Krantz.'

'Preston. Now all of a sudden you give me two plays in one night?'

Krantz turned to the doorman, 'It's O.K., Biff. Thanks.'

Biff took the hint and walked a few paces away.

'Well, you didn't get me out here to buy you a drink.'

'Right. Did you happen to notice who I was with tonight?' I asked.

'I saw the lady. I know her name, too,

but you'll excuse me if I don't use it.'

His tone was guarded.

'You've got it wrong, Krantz. This is strictly business.'

There was no telling from that impassive face whether he believed me or not. I decided probably not.

'The guy at the table, Harry Swenson. You know him, too?'

'I might. What's this all about?'

'I told you, it's business.'

He grinned.

'Sure, you told me. What you didn't tell me, but what everybody knows, is that some of your business is strange business. Dangerous business. My business is running a respectable place.'

'This is a respectable place?' I twitted. 'It's a tourist trap.'

'So it's a tourist trap. But it's a legitimate business. How long do you think I'd stay open if I started running a gossip column as well?'

I was disappointed, but not too much. Krantz's attitude was what I'd half expected.

'So you can't help me, huh?'

He shook his head.

'Sorry, Preston. Ask me about the club business. I'm a mine of information. On anything else I'm strictly D and D.'

'Never mind. See you.'

I went and got back into the car. As I pushed the button to start the motor, Krantz suddenly leaned his head in at the window Dixie had left open.

'That Biff has the biggest ears in town,' he told me. 'I don't know much about Swenson, but what I know I don't like. And he knows some funny people. Like tough people. Watch him.'

'Thanks.' I replied, but he was already walking back towards the club.

7

It was now almost eleven. There was time for one more visit before I called it a day. The clothes I had on would look a little out of place where I was going so I went back to the Parkside Towers. Here I put on my sharpest suit, a Hawaiian shirt and a loud tie. This outfit, plus a pair of chocolate and cream sport shoes that I bought for visits of this kind, made me into a regular gorgeous Gary. I hoped I wouldn't see anybody who knew me as I slipped out of the building, and I was lucky.

I drove down to Mike's Bar. The place was half-empty, a group of truck drivers having a noisy discussion at one end of the counter. Some of the booths were occupied, mostly by couples. They were having discussions too, only quieter. Very much quieter. I looked at the booth at the far end where Hudson had talked to the fatso. It was now occupied by a guy who'd taken on more booze than he could handle. There was a dame with him, a redhead with black roots to her hair. From the way they were silently struggling it was my guess she'd taken on more guy than she could handle.

'Beats the wrestling, huh?'

A large sad-faced man in a soiled white apron leaned on the bar counter from the business side. I nodded.

'Sure does. Say, I'll have a beer.'

While he filled the foaming glass I drummed on the counter with my finger tips, whistling aimlessly. He set the beer down in front of me. I leaned towards him in a conspiratorial way.

'Say, a friend of time told me to look up a certain party in here.'

He looked even sadder.

'Zasso? What party?'

'Name of Jo-Ann. My friend said she was a big blonde. Man, I'm for big blondes.' I looked puzzled. 'Funny thing he told me she serves the drinks in this place. But you're the only one I can see. And, no offence, but I don't go for you at all. Get it?'

I peeled off an inane laugh at this witty delivery, and nudged him with my elbow. He grinned his bartending grin, the one he'd had to learn to prevent him from tossing humourists out on their can.

'Your friend had it almost right, mister. But Jo-Ann don't work nights. Daytimes you'll find her.'

'Oh,' I made a face. 'Real dirty shame. I don't get to town much. Leaving again first thing tomorrow. Say, you don't think you might know another little girl who's lonely tonight, huh?'

He took a cloth and mopped at some spilled beer.

'I don't know what gives you an idea like that, mister. This is just a bar.'

'Well, no harm done. Guess I must have got the wrong idea from what Gregg said.'

'Who?'

'My friend. That guy who told me to look up this Jo-Ann.'

He nodded patiently.

'Sure, yeah. But the name. What was that name you said again?'

'Gregg,' I repeated. 'Gregg Hudson.

You must know him. Told me he comes in here a lot.'

'Just a minute.'

He threw the swab on to a metal tray and stepped through a door behind the bar.

'Mike,' he called.

There was some movement behind the door and the bartender talked to someone out of sight for about a minute. Then he stepped back inside and closed the door.

'Hey, we're all dying of thirst down here. 'Bout a little service, huh? 'Bout that?'

One of the truckies was banging on the counter with a huge hand. Signalling to me to wait, the bartender went down to save a few lives. I tasted the beer. It was a little better than the stuff they'd been peddling during the afternoon. Presently the door at the back opened and a man stepped out. I got a little tingle of excitement as I recognised Hudson's friend, the fat guy.

He stood, looking round, saw me and wandered up to where I was standing.

'I'm Mike,' he said, a wide smile on his face. 'I own the joint.'

'Well, well, well,' I replied heartily. 'The boss man in person. Real nice of you to bother about me.'

'I'm a real nice sort of fellow,' he assured me. 'And it's no bother at all. Least, I don't think it will be.'

Close up it was easy to see how thin the veneer of good humour was. The small creases downward from the corners of his smiling mouth, the pouched bags beneath his eyes, hinted at a face which in repose would look only evil. At the moment it was all pushed into that determined jolly expression which so many people associate with fat.

'You got a rule about drinking with the customers?' I queried.

'Yup. Otherwise I'd have been dead of the D.Ts years ago.' Then he changed the subject suddenly. 'That right you're a buddy of Hudson's?'

I made a face to indicate modesty.

'Wouldn't say 'buddy' exactly. I know him though, we have a few laughs and like that. You know.'

'Sure,' he nodded. 'Seen him lately?'

'Why, no. Fact is, I been outta town. Just got back this afternoon. I'm a travelling man, myself. Myers is the name, Chuck Myers.'

'Glad to know you, Chuck,' beamed Mike extending a pudgy paw.

'In town long?'

I wagged my head.

'Shouldn't be here at all. Few miles off my route in fact. But I got to thinking about this big blonde Gregg told me about and I thought, 'Chuck, boy, never mind the miles. Tonight we live a little'.' I let my face sag into despondency. 'Only we don't, it seems.'

The fat man patted me on the arm.

'Don't worry about it, Chuck. Maybe something'll turn up. Tell you what, you're all alone. Right?'

'Right.'

'So for lonely guys I got a special bottle in the back. Step through and sample a little something.'

I brightened up and winked at him knowingly. This was to tell him that Chuck Myers wasn't born yesterday.

135

Chuck knew what time it was. That 'special bottle' bit didn't fool old Chuck. He knew there'd maybe turn out to be a little lady out there just hoping a travelling man might drop by.

Mike winked back, obscene things happening to his eye pouches, and lifted the flap of the counter. I went through and followed him to the door. He led the way into a narrow passage stacked high with cartons of bottles. At the end of the passage was another door. He nodded towards it.

'Private office. C'mon.'

He led me into a small room which featured one desk, two chairs one leather one wood, and a liquor cabinet.

'Shut the door, will you? Don't want any nosy people bustin' into the party.'

He went round the desk as I turned to close the door. When I turned back he was sitting in the leather chair smiling a wide smile. In one fat hand was an Italian machine-pistol which wasn't smiling at all.

'Let's have a little talk, Chuck.'

I tried to look frightened. It wasn't hard.

'What is this?' I stammered. 'I don't have more than about forty dollars with me — '

'Never mind the forty dollars,' he beamed. 'It'll help towards the hospital bill.'

'H-hospital bill?'

'Sure. The one you're going to. Tell me what it's all about, Chuck?'

'I don't get it,' I said, still scared.

'You don't yet. But you'll get it, all right, if you don't talk it up. What're you doing here?'

'Like I told you, Gregg said to look up this mouse — '

'Mouse, schmouse,' he snarled. 'You're a liar. Hudson never told you anything of the kind. There's a thousand places in this town for picking up dames. This is the last place Hudson woulda sent you.'

'Well look, if I made a mistake I'm sorry,' I trembled. 'There's no need for that kind of thing.'

I pointed a shaking finger at the pistol. Mike laughed. His belly bounced around in the chair.

'You made a mistake all right, thinking

this was the bush league. I don't know what you're up to, Chuck, but I'm sure as hell gonna find out before you leave here.'

With his free hand he pulled the black telephone towards him, lifted the receiver and began to dial. He didn't take his eyes off me.

'I'm calling some people,' he advised me. 'You look kinda well-built, and I ain't the right shape for this kind of work. You could probably take me if I hadn't got this.' He waved the cannon. 'These people though, they're not like me. They're real hard guys. You'll talk when they get here.'

I said nothing. Finally he got his connection.

'Mike,' he announced. 'Is he there? It's important.'

There was a brief wait while the man at the other end got whoever it was. And whoever it was, there was a change in Mike's tone when he spoke to him.

'Sorry to call at this time of night — yeah — sure — well, there's this guy I got here. Calls himself Chuck Myers — no, neither did I, but he's pitchin'

138

some yarn about Hudson sent him here. Told him it was a girlie — drop. — No, that's what I figured — Yup, here right now. He's not going anywhere — no — you know I'll do whatever you say — yeah. G'bye.'

He put the receiver down carefully, waiting for the click that would tell him the other man had broken the connection first. On the fat face there was a glistening film of sweat. The man at the other end must have quite a lot of influence to induce such respect in a character like Mike.

He recovered some of his composure, even managed to smile again.

'Two guys on their way for a little friendly talk,' he informed me cheerfully. 'About Hudson. He got knocked off this afternoon.'

I registered surprise.

'But that's terrible — ' I began.

'Ain't it, though? There's some people, important people, want to know who did it. Couldn't have been you, huh, Chuck? Or the guys who sent you here?'

Suddenly I dropped the pretence. All

the good humour left his face as he noticed the change in my expression. I said.

'All right, you win. How long before these mugs get here?'

'Five minutes, maybe ten. Why?'

'This is big business, Mike. Let me outta here you get a yard.'

'A thousand bucks? You're crazy, these guys'd kill me.'

But he was listening. His eyes had narrowed at the thought of the money. I went up to the desk, showing agitation that wasn't entirely forced.

'All right, two thousand. Think of it.' I moved as close as I dared.

'Just turn your back for thirty seconds and you pick up twenty one hundred dollar bills. And there could be more, plenty more, for just a little of the right information.'

I was close to him now, not three feet from the uncompromising black muzzle of the gun. It was in his right hand, the telephone lay close to his left. I leaned towards the phone, beginning to reach for it.

'Let me call somebody — ' I began.

'Like hell,' he snarled, clamping his hand over mine.

Automatically his eyes swivelled to the left. My own left hand was now only inches from the side of the gun. I swept sideways hard. The gun was forced away towards the wall and his thick finger squeezed automatically. The steel-jacketed slug roared and plunked into the wall high near the ceiling. I had no grip on his gun arm, no way of preventing the inevitable swing back in my direction. He was frightened now, frightened and angry. A man who would kill. It wasn't the time for rules. With my right hand I snatched up the telephone and smashed it into the fat flabby face. He gave an awful scream as he tilted over backwards in the chair. I leaped over the desk and dived for the hand with the gun. Before his head crunched against the rear wall I had my hand clamped over the barrel of the gun. It could still kill me and he was still holding it, fat finger curled around the trigger inside the guard. There wasn't time for discussion. I pushed the barrel away from me with a vicious jerk. There was a splintering crack as the bone in his finger shattered and another wild scream of agonised rage from the man on the floor. I shook the useless finger free and whirled round as the door flew open. The bartender came rushing in.

'What's all the — ?'

The words shrivelled on his lips as he saw his boss pulling himself above the desk, his face a bloody pulp. Then he half-started for me, a doubtful look on the sad face. I brought up the pistol and shook my head.

'This is a gun, friend. I don't want to have to kill you with it. Back against the wall.'

Slowly he retreated, undecided whether he ought to try for me.

'Don't,' I told him. 'Just turn around and nobody'll get hurt.'

He faced the wall. Mike was half-lying across the desk, sobbing.

'Tell your boss the real big guys are interested in this operation,' I said. 'The only reason I'm not knocking you off right now is so's you'll pass the message.'

He said nothing and I turned for the door. From where he was sprawled Mike was watching me from his one good eye. The other was a mess of blood. Checking the passage quickly, I stepped out of the room pulling the door shut and turning the key. Then I shoved the machine-pistol into my side pocket and went back into the bar. Nobody took any special notice of me as I headed for the entrance and out into the street. I walked to where I'd left the car, climbed in and settled down, watching the front of Mike's Bar. I hadn't long to wait. Within five minutes a long black limousine swept smoothly to a halt outside. Two men climbed out hurriedly, slamming the doors. Instantly the car pulled away again, nosed its way back into traffic and was gone. The two men strode briskly across the sidewalk looking neither to left nor right. As they moved under the lights I recognised one, a small-time muscle boy named Bice Smirnoff. The other man was a stranger, except that I knew the type. Big, broad-shouldered, with a brutish face and an awkward swinging movement to his body. A typical hard gee, a man I would expect to see calling on an inconvenient character who'd pushed his nose into the wrong place. A man I would expect to see in company with Bice Smirnoff. Bice was a wrestler onetime, a sticks-circuit pro with little to offer but the ability to take punishment and show off his bulging biceps. Which is how he came by the name. I was thinking about him as I coasted away back to Parkside. Bice was nobody, a nothing, a typical racket fringe character who'd do anything anybody told him. Anybody who had the price. It was the anybody I was interested in, the one who was prepared to spend money on hiring two thugs to rough up a stranger who mistakenly thought a drinking bar was a pick-up bar. It seemed like a lot of trouble to take.

When I got home I quickly shed the Chuck Myers outfit. Padding around in my shorts I put on some coffee to brew, and sat down by the telephone. I wanted to know where I could get hold of Bice Smirnoff, and in Monkton City you want to know something like that you call up

144

Charlie Surprise. Charlie is the original reference guide for information of that kind. Names, addresses, who's working with who, who's gunning for who, Charlie has it all. He wasn't at the first two places I tried. Finally I ran him to earth at a trap called the Birds Nest.

'Who is this?' he enquired, full of suspicion.

'Old friend,' I told him. 'Preston, remember?'

'I remember,' he said cautiously. 'Kinda late isn't it?'

'It's late,' I agreed. 'But you're the one who's still out living it up. I'm at home.'

'Living it up?' he snorted. 'Listen, I'm working. If I don't raise two hundred by the first race tomorrow, Keppler's gonna put me on the list.'

He was almost beside himself with worry and I could understand that. Charlie plays the horses. Sometimes he wins, sometimes he loses. Especially sometimes he loses. The point is he plays every race on the cards, every day. His whole life hinges on the unpredictable quadrupeds with the opera-star temperaments. If Keppler put Charlie on the list it meant he wouldn't be able to place a bet practically anywhere in the state. And in that event he might just as well be dead.

'Say, I'm sorry to hear that, Charlie,' I meant it. 'There's a tenspot coming your way in return for a simple piece of information.'

'Ten, you say?'

He was definitely interested. In Charlie's world ten dollars can be turned into a bigger fortune than two hundred bucks in a very short space of time. It was a straw and Charlie was at the clutching stage. I could almost hear him working out the details.

'I'm interested in Bice Smirnoff. Want to know where he lives.'

'I don't know,' he said, doubtfully. 'That Bice is kinda rough. He might just tear off my ears with his teeth. I don't know, Preston.'

'If Keppler puts you on the list,' I reminded him. 'What will you need with ears?'

'Yeah,' he sounded glum. 'Ain't it the truth. How about Bice? You gonna give him to the law, or anything?'

'I just want him to answer a couple of questions. Small questions. I'll even tell you what they are, if you want.'

I knew that would stampede Charlie, and it did.

'No,' he said quickly. 'No, thanks. I don't want to know anything about it. People around this town, they know things, they get hurt. Don't tell me nothing about it. Just take the address. He has a pad down on Vine Street over a dirty spoon.'

I wrote it down.

'Who runs the spoon?'

'Guy named Max. You can forget him, he's strictly nowhere. Not tied in with Bice, if that's what you're thinking.'

'The thought had crossed my mind,' I admitted. 'One more little thing, Charlie. You got any ideas about who's paying Bice's laundry bills lately?'

'No. I probably wouldn't tell you if I did, but I don't know. Way I hear it Bice does whatever needs doing for anybody.'

'Or to anybody,' I interjected.

'That too. Well that's it, Preston. How

do I pick up the ten?'

I told him the name of a man who'd give him ten on my say so and rang off. The coffee was about ready. I poured some of the scalding liquid into a cup, leaving a good space unfilled. Then I took a hefty slug of imported whisky and filled the space. The wondrous bouquet of hot coffee and whisky began to float about the room. I sat down in a deep chair, put the cup within easy reach. Then I lit an Old Favourite, leaned back and began to pick over my meagre stock of facts. There weren't really enough of them to qualify as a stock.

A Mexican girl named Juanita Morales hops over the border and makes for Monkton City. She gets a job as housemaid or thereabouts to Mrs. Floyd Whitton Junior, on the recommendation of one Gregg Hudson. Hudson can't or won't remember how he met her. After a few months Juanita walks out of the job because she's pregnant. Her father gets worried so he dodges the border patrol too, and hires one private investigator to find her. Through Mrs. Whitton, the investigator questioned Hudson, who led to a fat saloon keeper named Mike. Mike led to a tourist agency run by Myron C. Hartley. The investigator, me, talked with Hartley. A few hours later up turn two candidates for the freshman-of-the-year title. They lead to Juanita who confesses what happened to her. End of Story. Only it wasn't. Somewhere along the line somebody rubbed out Gregg Hudson, and somebody sent two thugs to beat up a travelling salesman who mentioned Hudson's name to Mike the saloon keeper. And Mrs. Floyd Whitton, who was at the beginning of the trail, had been drinking with a reputed tough character named Swenson, who turned out to be drinking also with Myron C. Hartley. And the two freshmen worked for Hartley too.

I thought about them all again, and the more I thought about it, the more confused it became. I worked out the most elaborate theories in an attempt to relate any of them to the facts and names I had. Most of the theories started out well enough, but always left two or three people unexplained. And certainly I didn't come up with anything that would tell me why a man should get himself murdered just because he happened once to find work for a girl who later got herself in trouble. One thing emerged from all the brain exercise. Practically everybody in town seemed to know more about this deal than I did.

By the time I'd almost finished the coffee I was completely relaxed. Able to see things in their proper perspective. I'd been getting all excited about nothing at all. So I happened to talk to a guy named Hudson on the very same day somebody killed him. Hudson probably talked to a dozen other people today. Were they all fretting around at this hour of the night worrying about who was responsible? Certainly not. I had been paid one hundred dollars to find a girl whose father was worried. I found her and that was that. Tomorrow I would tell her father the yarn Juanita and I had agreed, bundle him back to Baja California, and that would be the end of the incident. We have a perfectly efficient police department here in this city, run on the taxes extorted from innocent citizens like me. Why shouldn't they do a little work once in a while? What I ought to do was get a good night's rest, and forget the whole thing. Permanently.

I don't even remember drinking the rest of the coffee before I fell sound asleep in the chair.

8

I crawled out around eight in the morning. While the coffee was brewing I cleaned up and made myself presentable enough to be seen on the street. Then I swallowed some of the black liquid, wolfed a slice of toast and went out. Pop Kline was opening up his store for the day when I walked in.

'Where is he, Pop?' I asked.

He pointed to the back of the store.

'In there some place. You going to take him away from here perhaps?'

I paused.

'Why, Pop? Has he been a lot of trouble?'

'No,' he shrugged. 'It isn't that exactly. Just that a man gets used to living alone. When you been doing it enough years you get so Saint Peter himself would get on your nerves if you had to live in the same house with him.'

'Sure, I understand. And I'm grateful

152

to you for having him at all. He should be leaving tonight.'

Pop nodded, and went on unlocking the windows. I wandered through to the back and found old Morales hunched in a corner, smoking a yellow cigarette. His glum expression vanished when he saw me.

'Ah, señor. Señor Preston, you have found my little girl, huh? You take me to her?'

He scrambled to his feet, all eagerness.

'Well, yes in a way. Yes and no,' I began.

'Señor?'

Naturally he could make little sense of what I'd said. Looking at that eager, trusting face I was not enthusiastic about what I had to do. I went into my routine about Juanita and her mythical friend. Once I got into my stride I got more confident. After all if Morales was going to buy, he was entitled to as good a pitch as I could give him. I told him a very nice little story. When I reached the end it was a disappointment to hear no crescendo violins. He swallowed it, the whole thing. It was a good story. There was only one

153

tough question, and I was ready for that.

'Gracias,' he nodded. 'Eet is good. Now I will thank only thees frien' of Juanita, and I go back home.'

'Er, well I'm afraid it isn't going to be possible for you to talk to her, Mr. Morales,' I said hesitantly, inviting more questions.

'So? Why not, señor?'

'Well, this is a little bit embarrassing, but I'll have to give it to you straight. You see, this friend, the one I talked to, she wanted to know why I was interested in Juanita. She said how did she know she wasn't going to get Juanita into trouble if she talked to me. And she made it very clear that in that case she wouldn't talk to me at all.'

He nodded with satisfaction.

'A true friend. Such a friend as I would weesh for my Juanita. What has thees to do with my talking to her now?'

I looked earnest.

'That's it. When I told her I was working for Juanita's father she said O.K. I could have the story. But when I told her about you, about how you hadn't any papers and that was why you couldn't go around asking questions, she almost had a fit. You see this girl, Juanita's friend, she has a father too. A public official, a man of the highest character. If anybody found out his daughter was friendly with an illegal immigrant — you'll excuse the expression — it could be the end of her father's career. So I'm sorry, Mr. Morales. It's out of the question.'

He nodded again.

'A fine lady, she must be. To protect first my Juanita, then her own father, such a one is a friend.'

'I was hoping you'd look at it that way,' I said gently.

We arranged that he would leave Monkton that night as soon as it was dark. I told him a friend of mine would drive him to the border at a spot where he could dodge the patrols. After that he'd have to find his own way home. The old man was overjoyed at what he called such kindness. Finally after a lot of handshaking and one or two tears from the Mexican, I left.

My next call was to the office. Florence

Diby was cool in a crisp white blouse.

'Good morning, Mr. Preston,' she was very formal. 'I hardly expected you so soon. Perhaps the lady's appearance didn't match up with her voice.'

'Lady? Voice?' I shook my head. 'You'll have to spell it, Miss Digby. I don't function too fast at this hour.'

'You didn't get a telephone call at your apartment?'

'Uh uh. What's it all about?'

'It was about a half hour ago. I'd only been in the office a few minutes. This girl telephoned and wanted to talk to you. Said she was desperate. She certainly sounded as if she meant it, so I gave her your Parkside number. She said she'd call you right away.'

It was clear that Florence didn't entirely believe me.

'I was already out and about,' I explained. 'Maybe I'll hang on here for a while, see if she calls again. I needn't ask if she left a name?'

'Sorry, no name,' returned Florence Digby.

I telephoned around until I located

Charlie Surprise. For fifty dollars he finally agreed to drive Morales down to the border that evening. Shortly after we finished talking I got another call. Miss Digby said,

'It's her again.'

'Fine, put her on.'

I waited, then a voice said,

'Is that Mark Preston?'

It was one of those voices some women develop for talking to men with. It was soft and silky, somehow suggestive. For me at nine-thirty in the morning it hadn't any appeal.

'Who is this?' I asked.

'Mr. Preston. I want to talk to you and I may not have much time to do it. Where can I see you?'

'What's wrong with here in my office?'

'No. If anybody saw me calling on you they might misunderstand.'

'Or do you mean they might understand too well?' I suggested.

'Have it any way you like.'

There was something about the voice that was hitting a familiar note. I'd talked to this girl before.

'Do you know the Bahia Apartments?'

'On West Shore? Yup.'

'Number 24. I could meet you there in thirty minutes. It's important.'

Despite the languorous tone which had been practised to a point where it was now habit, this girl was worried.

'One question, Miss Mystery. Just give me the slightest reason why I should be interested.'

There was a pause.

'All right. You might learn something about Gregg Hudson,' she replied.

'Thirty minutes,' I confirmed.

West Shore is a sheltered inlet at the Beach end of town. Here there was no commercialism permitted to spoil either the scenery or the quiet luxury of those who could afford the fare. There was just one hotel, one night-club, one excellent and expensive restaurant. There were a couple of dozen top-income private homes and the exclusive Bahia Apartments. My lady friend either had money or she had friends who had money. As I opened up along the coast highway I was inclined to vote for the second alternative.

The Bahia Apartments nestled at the foot of a cliff. Tucked discreetly away behind a line of palm trees the place gave off an expensive atmosphere almost before you got close. Number 24 was at ground level and on a corner. I climbed out of the car and inspected the place. There was only one way in or out of the apartment, discounting windows, and that was by way of the bright yellow door. There were several other cars in the fore-court and I had no way of telling whether they went with Apartment 24 or not. The .38 was hard and comforting against my chest as I rang the bell. The door opened almost at once.

'Come in.'

It was the blonde receptionist I'd seen in Hartley's office the day before. Today she wore a lime green suit, severely cut, and she was just as beautiful as I'd thought the first time. A man could be forgiven if he forgot to do anything else but stare at her as she walked back into the room. A man could get dead doing it, too. I slipped the police special into my right hand and checked behind the door.

'What on earth are you doing?' she demanded.

I didn't answer. I went through the apartment thoroughly until I was satisfied there weren't any little surprises in store. Like muscle hiding in a cupboard for instance. Then I went back to the door and slipped the catch.

'Satisfied?' asked Blondie sarcastically.

I shrugged.

'Lady, you wouldn't believe how many guys get their brains beaten out of them just because they got careless around a beautiful girl like you.'

'Oh, yes I would believe it,' she returned. 'And I don't blame you for being suspicious.'

I put the gun away.

'This your place?'

'No. It belongs to — a friend. This friend doesn't use it very much, and I happened to know it was empty at the moment.'

She sat herself down, smoothing the skirt carefully into place over the showgirl legs. I sat too and offered her an Old Favourite. After we'd lit them I said,

'Well, here we are. Do I get a name now?'

'Of course. Sylvia Le Fay. It isn't my real name, but I've used it a long time. Nobody else in this town would know me by any other.'

'O.K., Sylvia, what's the big problem?'

She'd been studying me, making mental notes. I've seen people do it before, and it usually means they're making up their minds how far to trust me. Sylvia was no exception.

'You remember me?' she queried.

'That has to be a joke,' I replied. 'You never met the man who'd forget you in twenty-four hours.'

She smiled faintly, a lazy curl of smoke escaping from the red lips.

'I've asked about you,' she informed me. 'People tell me to trust you.'

'What people?' I countered.

'Never mind. I believe I can trust you. The trouble is, I'm not certain how much I want you to know.'

'Because it might mean you could be in trouble with the law?' I suggested.

'It could indeed. Plenty of trouble.' Her

face was worried.

'I see. So where do we go from here. You obviously mean to tell me some of it. For example, you mentioned Gregg Hudson.'

Her brow clouded, and she drew a little harder on the cigarette.

'How well did you know Gregg?' she demanded.

'Not at all. From what I hear I didn't miss anything.'

She grinned again, but it wasn't pleasant to see that beautiful mouth twisted into such cynical lines.

'You hear wrong. You did miss something. You missed the biggest louse on the Pacific Coast. Gregg was something new in four-flushing whore-chasers. Believe me, I've been around, but Gregg was a new experience.'

I nodded.

'Are you speaking from personal experience?'

'Of course, that's why we're here,' she seemed surprised at the question.

'I was wondering about that,' I confessed. 'If you're going to tell me you killed the man I'll be sorry about it, but it won't stop me going to the police.'

She shook her head.

'It isn't that. You see, I'm afraid. I lived with him, with Gregg, for a few months. I knew a good deal about him, knew all his rotten little ways.'

I thought I began to see where she was heading.

'So you think you might know who did kill him?'

She inclined her head.

'I can think of more than one person. Besides me, that is.'

'Then you shouldn't be talking to me,' I said flatly. 'You want the Monkton City Police Department.'

'No, I couldn't do that. A lot of people would suffer, if I did. People who trust me. I can't explain that to you, but you'll just have to take my word.'

'Why should I? None of this means a thing to me,' I told her.

'Would five hundred dollars mean anything to you?' She dived into a crocodile purse and produced a wad of bills.

'Well now,' I said slowly. 'Not if it meant suppressing evidence in a case of murder.'

She thrust the bills towards me.

'I'm hiring you.'

'At what, exactly?'

'Let's say as my agent in Monkton City. Look Preston, let's talk frankly. You must have seen girls like me before, plenty. I'm a good-timer. I like the bright lights, the expensive apartments, the good green dollar. If a girl wants all that she needs two things, good looks and a close mouth. I've got the looks and I have a reputation for keeping my mouth shut. I'm no lily. Some of the things I've seen might surprise even you, but everybody knows they can trust Sylvia. At least everybody thought so till now.'

She broke off, biting her lip.

'Now? What's so different about now?' I queried.

'Gregg's murder, naturally. I'm not sure who killed Gregg, and I don't much care. But it won't be long before the police find out I was living with him just a couple of months ago. When they get to

164

me, they might think I'm a good suspect. Let's face it, I am.'

I agreed with that.

'I don't follow all this,' I told her. 'Naturally the police will suspect you, ask questions. But if you didn't do it, you've got nothing to fear.'

'From the police, no,' she agreed. 'But it'll be a different story with everybody else. People will worry about what I'm liable to say.'

'They never worried before,' I reminded her.

'That's true. It's also true that I was never a suspect in a murder before. Remember, only two people can be sure it wasn't me who killed him. The murderer and me. Everybody else probably wonders whether I did it or not.'

'So?'

'So they'll also be wondering what I might say. Whether I might try to make a deal with the police. Tell what I know about this, that and the other. For what I know any District Attorney would be glad to trade a man-slaughter indictment.'

I ground out the cigarette.

'You wouldn't care to tell me, I guess?'

'You guess right. The point is do you see the spot I'm in? Just because of what I know any one of a number of people might think it was too risky to have me walking around.'

She could have been exaggerating but I doubted it. If she really was involved in anything big, and it had to be big for so many others to be mixed up in it. Sylvia Le Fay represented a risk to those people. People who run big operations can't afford to take chances and they certainly wouldn't trust their safety to a girl who was a strong murder suspect.

'All right,' I nodded. 'I'll go along. From what you've told me, which incidentally is not much, I'd say it isn't healthy where you live. And just exactly where does that get you, and why am I here?'

'You're going to save my life, Preston.'

She dabbed out her cigarette in a nervous flurry of red sparks.

'Can I have another smoke?'

As I lit it for her she said,

'I'm getting out. Clean out of this

166

town. I daren't tell anybody where I'm going. The only people I know are likely to talk if they get any pressure, and that won't help me at all. So I tell nobody. Except you.'

It seemed to be an invitation to say something.

'Why me? If you're bucking the big action don't drag me into it, baby.'

'You needn't worry,' she said scornfully. 'Nobody'll know I even talked to you. All you do is remember where to find me. When they catch the guy who killed Gregg Hudson you let me know. Then I come back, explain to everybody what happened. If necessary you can back up my story. Nobody gets hurt.'

It could work, I reflected. There was only one detail I didn't care for. If Sylvia had killed Hudson herself, I would be helping a murderer to escape from the law. No, that was ridiculous. If she was guilty she didn't have to do this duet with me at all. By now she could be on the way to South America, and have saved five hundred dollars into the bargain.

'And that's all I have to do? No alibis,

buying phoney passports, stuff like that?'

'Nothing like that.'

She gazed at me out of the worried hazel eyes. I sighed,

'O.K. What's the address?'

She told me the name of a small hotel in Sacramento. I pushed the wad of bills into my wallet and stood up.

'This is really worth all this money?' I asked. 'I'd have been overpaid at twenty-five bucks.'

'Maybe, from your point of view,' she agreed. 'But then, it isn't your life, is it, Preston?'

She had me there. She walked to the door. Watching her I wondered what it was Hudson had that would net him a dame like that.

'I'll leave first if you don't mind,' she said. 'Just in case you thought of hiding along the road somewhere and following me. I have to make one call before I leave town. A private call.'

The door was open and she stood in the bright sunlight, half-turned towards me.

'Remember, Preston, I'm relying on you.'

'I'll remember.'

She smiled and pulled the door shut. Then there was a scrape and some clicking. Sylvia took no chances on being followed. I was locked in. From the window I saw her climb into a small black convertible and drive away. That left me.

When the car was out of sight I thought about how I was going to break out of the apartment without attracting attention. It would be a simple matter to climb out of a window, not so simple to explain to any inquisitive passer-by what I was doing there in the first place. I didn't even know the owner's name. I searched the apartment again, this time to see if there was any information lying around that I ought to have. The place was as impersonal as a hotel room. It would have been no surprise to find a Gideon Bible. The apartment didn't seem to be used very much, though there was shaving stuff in the little blue cabinet on the bathroom wall. The giant refrigerator was empty, and there was a thin film of dust over some cups I found.

Then there came a sharp rap at the

door. I went to it and stood there wondering. Again the rap, followed by a cheerful voice.

'Excelsior, sir.'

'Who is that?' I said through the door.

'Excelsior, sir. Your coffee.'

'Oh.' I tried to sound as though that made everything all right. 'I can't open the door, it's stuck.'

A key grated in the lock and the door opened. A tow-haired kid in a suit of white silk overalls stood there, a tray in one hand. With the other he held out a key.

'Left the key in the lock, sir.'

I took the key and looked sheepish. Then I took the tray.

'I didn't order any coffee,' I told him.

'No, sir, that's right. It was a lady's voice on the phone. She said ten-thirty.' He looked anxious, 'You do want it don't you?'

'Sure,' I grinned, 'I want it.'

I gave him five dollars, and waited for him to mention change.

'Thank you, sir. Thank you very much.'

Then he was gone, whistling. I could

whistle for my change. I dumped the tray on a table and left. Sylvia Le Fay seemed to be a very thorough girl, I reflected. I liked the move with the coffee. It had been timed almost to the moment when I would have had to take a chance of some sort to get out of Apartment 24. And it also gave Sylvia a chance to gain too much of a lead for me to catch her, even if I'd wanted to. I headed into town.

9

The desk sergeant at police headquarters inspected me as if hoping to spot something he could arrest me for. He didn't like me a bit.

'Randall in?' I queried.

'Detective Sergeant Randall is out on a call,' he informed me. 'What did you want to see him for?'

The desk man was a new face to me.

'I'm a stool pigeon,' I told him. 'You know we never talk to anybody but our contacts. Randall is my boy.'

His face took on an expression of loathing.

'Then you'd best beat it, creep. He ain't here.'

I looked worried.

'This is kind of urgent. Maybe I'll talk to Rourke.'

It was his turn to look worried.

'Lieutenant Rourke? Of Homicide? Brother, he eats guys like you.'

'His stomach must be in terrible shape. Tell him I'm here. Preston.'

'If this is a gag — ' he warned.

'No gag. Tell him.'

He lifted the instrument and pressed a white key from a row at his side.

'Lieutenant? Desk. Say I have one of Randall's stoolies here. Says he wants to talk to you. Name of Preston — I see — yes, Lieutenant.'

His ears were red.

'A comic, huh. Go on up. Oh, and comic — ' he leaned over slightly. 'I'll remember you.'

I grinned at him and went upstairs. Now and then you read articles in magazines about the fine new police headquarters in Squareville, Nebraska. Plenty of lay-out stuff, mezzanine flooring, brand new equipment, shots of the white marble steps etc. etc. Reading about Squareville is the nearest we ever get to a decent police building in Monkton City. Stuck off the main heart of the City, in surroundings more conducive to crime than crime prevention, the harassed officers of our overworked force are subjected to every conceivable inconvenience in their work. Badly-lit offices, over-crowding, worn-out furniture. The sanitation alone would raise the public health banner in any other official premises. But anything would do for the law-boys, that was the clear message from the administration. And, of the available accommodation, the Bureau of Homicide rated just three rooms on the third floor. One for interrogations, briefings etc., one for the plain clothes officers, one for the lieutenant and his sergeant. This was the third door along, and was clearly stamped as the one that mattered by its possession of a half-panel in dirty frosted glass. I knocked and went in. John Rourke sat behind a battered desk glowering at me.

'Before you say anything at all, Preston, get this. The police in this town have got more to do with their time than play Amos 'n Andy with you. You ride that desk sergeant again and I'll personally break your leg.'

'He said your stomach was in bad shape,' I observed. 'But let's not quarrel, John — '

'Don't you John me. Lieutenant Rourke to you and don't you forget it.'

It was one of those Lieutenant Rourke days evidently. I went and parked on a rickety chair strategically situated between the two desks. The idea was that both Rourke and Randall could blast at the victim from opposite sides.

'You know, Preston, I'm disappointed.' Rourke stuck one of his evil little black cigars between his teeth, lit it, and fanned a yellow cloud of the stinging smoke towards me. 'We've had our little differences of opinion from time to time, but I don't remember you ever hid behind a woman's skirts before.'

'I don't think I follow you,' I said slowly.

With Rourke it never pays to assume you know what he's driving at. With him a statement can be a question, and a question can mean whatever he chooses. He'd been asking questions for thirty-five years, and ten thousand interviews have left him with little to learn about the procedure.

'You follow me,' he asserted. 'I'm

talking about you using Mrs. Whitton to stop Gil Randall from pestering you.'

'That's not the way I remember it. I recall Randall overhearing a private conversation. After that he made up his own mind.'

'Randall has a family to keep. He can't afford to throw away almost twenty years seniority just because he offends the biggest names in town.'

I nodded my agreement.

'True. Still, I didn't come down here to quarrel with you boys. Came to give you some information.'

'Give?' His eyes screwed up suspiciously. 'What's your end?'

'Nothing. Just a citizen aiding the cause of justice. I found out Hudson had a special girl friend, one who got a pretty rough ride. She could be the one you want.'

'Zasso? Name?' Rourke picked up a pencil.

'Sylvia Le Fay. She used to live with — '

My voice died away when I saw the weary expression on his face as he replaced the pencil beside his pad.

'Might have known it wouldn't be something any good. We know all about Miss Le Fay. Fact, that's where Randall is right now.'

'Where?'

'Gone down to where she works. He's going to bring her in here for a little chat.'

'I see. So I'm a bit late, huh?'

He smiled with satisfaction.

'A bit.' Then he picked up some notes and read aloud. 'Sylvia Le Fay, aged twenty-five. Blonde, natural. Height five five, weight approx. one hundred and twenty. One time showgirl and model. Now receptionist for tourist agency. You see.'

He tapped at the notes with his thick finger. Before I could reply the phone rang.

'Homicide. Lieutenant Rourke,' he said briskly. 'Oh Gil — Yes, I — What? — O.K. what have you done? — good — yup I'll fix that and be right over — Yeah.'

He slammed the instrument down and swore savagely.

'Too late. Little Sylvia has beat it.'

That wasn't any news to me, but the next part was.

'She left us a little something to remember her by. The guy she worked for ran an outfit called the M. City Tourist Agency. He's in the office now. Stretched out on the floor with guess what growing out of a kidney?'

'An ice pick,' I whispered slowly.

'Correct.'

Rourke grabbed at another phone and gave rapid instructions for the lab men and photographers to get over to the agency right away. Then he stood up and grabbed his hat.

'Oh, Lieutenant,' I got up from the chair. 'Any chance of my riding over there? I do have an interest.'

The fierce eyes raked over me.

'If I don't let you go you'll probably have Mrs. Whitton get my pension cancelled. Just behave yourself over there. Remember this is police business.'

He went down the stairs two at a time and ran out to the official car. For a man who is due for a pension in eight years, Rourke can certainly move around. I climbed into my own heap and swung around in a circle to fall in behind the police sedan as it nosed out into the traffic stream.

When we reached the building I hoped we wouldn't draw the elevator man who'd been so helpful to me the day before, and I was lucky. On the sixth floor there was chaos. The corridor leading to the M. City Tourist Agency offices was jammed with excited chattering people, all speculating, rumouring, generally making themselves a nuisance. A uniformed patrolman was doing his best to keep a gangway clear. Rourke scowled, selected an elderly man who looked somewhat distinguished in his dark business suit.

'You, sir, may I ask who you are?' enquired Rourke.

The man started, fiddled with his tie, cleared his throat.

'Why yes, I am Spencer Warren of Warren Commercial Enterprises.'

Rourke's only link with Ireland is the annual St. Patrick's Day Parade, but they never lose the blarney. He smiled widely.

'Yes, I thought your face was familiar. Even a police officer likes to keep in touch with the leading business figures in the community.'

Warren smiled deprecatingly, wallowing in the effect this conversation must be having on the tight-packed audience.

'Now, Mr. Warren, it's lucky you're here. I'd like to ask you as a public spirited citizen to use your influence here, and get these good people back where they belong. No doubt the other executives present will want to help too.'

A thickly built man of fifty or so spoke up.

'I am F. Proctor, sir, of Proctor Advertising. All my people will be back at their desks within two minutes.'

He glared at Warren, to show that an outfit like Proctor didn't need any lead in its demonstration of civic allegiance from people like him. Warren immediately began shepherding at a group of stenographers. By the time Rourke and I reached the outer office door of the M. City Tourist Agency the patrol officer was alone in the corridor.

'Don't know how you do it, Lieutenant,' I remarked.

He snorted.

'Course you don't. If you'd spent sixteen years pounding a beat like I did, you might have learned a lot of things you don't pick up leaning on bars.'

Inside the office another uniformed man stood close by the door. He gave Rourke a salute and looked at me curiously. Sylvia's desk didn't seem nearly so impressive without her sitting behind it. The other girl, the one with the coal-black hair, was slumped in a chair while a bald-headed man fussed around her. She was either unconscious or in shock.

'Lieutenant Rourke,' announced my companion, 'I'm from the Homicide Bureau.'

'Oh.' The bald man didn't look round. 'I'm Doctor Karel. This young woman is in mild shock.'

'In here, Lieutenant.'

Gil Randall appeared at the door of the manager's office and beckoned. He saw me and looked mildly surprised. Rourke moved towards his sergeant and I followed. Myron C. Hartley was stretched out on the soft wool carpeting, arms flung forward as though he'd been trying to reach something. The telephone rested on the desk three feet above the outstretched hands. To me it seemed he'd been trying to pull the phone down by tugging at the cord. I'd have given plenty to know what number he would have asked for. Not that it mattered to him any more. He was wearing the same suit of white linen that he'd worn yesterday, plus a little extra decoration at the back where the handle of an ice-pick stuck obscenely up in the air. The blood had stopped flowing some time back, and the huge stain of ugly red reminded me somehow of a target with the ice-pick acting as a bull's-eye. I didn't see his face until I moved further round, then I wished I hadn't. The eyes were open, frozen in pain-filled horror, while the mouth was twisted into a travesty of itself by the sudden agony of the thrust.

Rourke prowled around taking everything in.

'When did it happen?' he demanded.

'This morning, early,' Randall informed him. 'Could have been any time between seven-thirty and eleven.'

'Oh? Why?'

'Because the cleaning staff fixed the office just after seven and there was someone working in the corridor outside until seven-thirty. After that there's no satisfactory check until eleven o'clock. That's when Miss Schultz came in and found him.'

'Schultz?' Rourke's eyebrows lifted.

'The girl outside,' explained Randall. 'She works here. Eleven is the time she normally starts.'

'I should get a job like that,' grumbled Rourke.

You should look like Miss Schultz, I thought privately. But I didn't say anything. It wasn't the time.

'All right, Gil.' Rourke sat down in the padded leather chair behind the desk and produced one of his noxious weeds. 'Let's have the rest of it.'

'I came down here to pick up Miss Le Fay — ' began Randall, ' — oh, by the way I have an all-stations call out for her,

Lieutenant — well, I arrived here just after eleven. I found Miss Schultz in a state of collapse. When I found Hartley's body I put out the alarm for Le Fay and called you. Myron Cyril Hartley was aged forty-one. He's been running this agency since it started two years ago. He isn't married, and seems to be worth quite a lot of money. He has a house at the Beach end and a new car. Don't know yet why it is but he doesn't seem to keep his female receptionists very long. They mostly stay a few months then leave. Schultz has been here six months, Le Fay almost five.'

'Yup. What's this all about, this place? Trips to Honolulu, stuff like that?'

'A little. They seem to run all the regular tours and such. Mostly though they seem to concentrate on the convention trade. I had a quick look at some of the records. Hartley seems to have had a corner on conventions in this town. Way it looks to me if you want to run a banquet or a conference or anything, you just get hold of Hartley and he does the rest.'

'H'm. Doesn't sound much in our line, that part. I like the girls better. Much better. Here's a well-heeled bachelor who goes in for swell-looking receptionists. He doesn't keep 'em very long either. Suddenly one day someone plants an ice-pick in his back, and the latest receptionist goes missing. Doesn't seem to require a great big brain like mine to work out that one, does it?'

He forced twin streams of swirling brown smoke from his nostrils and glared at me.

'You didn't answer me, Preston. What could be easier than this one, eh?'

'Nothing, the way you're telling it, Lieutenant. Only you're leaving out a little point that may have a bearing here.'

He grinned wolfishly.

'Listen to this, Randall. You don't often get a chance to listen to a famous character like Preston. O.K. what's the point?'

I knew he was needling me. He knew exactly what I was going to say and so did Randall.

'It's simply that the story would hold together better if somebody hadn't also left one of those things sticking out of

185

Hudson yesterday.'

'Yeah. Complicates it, doesn't it?' agreed Rourke. 'You got any other ideas about all this, Preston? Without betraying any of Mrs. Whitton's confidences of course? By the way, you never did say which Mrs. Whitton it was did you?'

'No, I didn't,' I confirmed. 'And in answer to the question, yes, I may have a small idea taking shape. I'll get in touch with you later.'

Randall stepped lightly between me and the door and held out a restraining hand about the size of a small door.

'Don't hurry off,' he pleaded. 'Bring a little colour into the life of a poor police officer. Tell me about your theory.'

'It isn't a theory, Gil. It's not even a real idea. Just the beginning of one. I will tell you where I'm going though if you want. I'm going to have a talk with my client and tell her she's putting me in a difficult position with the police. I'm going to tell her that I'm getting the snotty treatment from guys I've known for years. Then I'm going to ask her if it's O.K. for me to tell you the few little things I know. I don't say they'll be any help to you, but at least I'll be trying.'

I said all this with a deadpan face. The face of an honest man who's protecting his client in the face of hostile officialdom. A man who was sacrificing the friendship of years for the sake of a professional code. It seemed to have some effect too. Randall dropped the enormous hand.

'Sorry, Preston, but this is murder, not a shortage in the tennis club subscriptions. I know you'll help us when you can. Just get around to it, will you?'

'Don't stand there blubbering over that fourflusher, Randall.' Rourke suddenly roared. 'And don't swallow all that fruit-juice about this guy having sealed lips and so on. The only thing keeping his mouth shut is somebody tying his lips together with gold thread. Now, you hear me, Preston. Mrs. Whitton or no Mrs. Whitton I'm giving you till tonight to co-operate with this department. Whatever you know, I want it. I'm giving you a break, leaving you the rest of the day to produce. After that you'll be hauled in on suspicion.'

I started to ask 'on suspicion of what' but Rourke saw it coming.

'And don't say 'of what'. Just on suspicion, that's all.'

I got out before he changed his mind and booked me on the spot. In the outer office the bald doctor was still trying to rouse the sole remaining representative of the M. City Tourist Agency. I rode down in the elevator and made for the row of pay-booths in the lobby, which was now full of reporters and camera-boys.

'Police,' said a man at the other end.

'Homicide.' I tried to make my voice gruff.

He switched me through.

'Homicide. Detective Manders.'

'Lemme talk to the lieutenant,' I growled.

'Lieutenant's out on a call,' he told me. 'Who is this?'

'A friend. Tell the lieutenant if he wants to know more about who's losing a lot of ice-picks, he ought to try Bice Smirnoff.'

'Smirnoff? I don't get it. What's this all about?' queried Manders.

'It's about murder, copper. Don't forget the name. Bice Smirnoff.'

Then I hung up. I knew that the detective would keep me talking as long as he could while the department tracked down the call. That was a chance I couldn't afford to take. I didn't think Bice had killed Hudson or Hartley, but he was certainly working for somebody who knew a lot about it. The police knew all about Bice. With a record like he had, they wouldn't think twice about hauling him in for a grilling. They might learn something and they might not, but either way Bice's employers would feel the law was coming a little too close. Something might give.

★　★　★

The Monkton City Globe occupies a grey stone building in the business section. The Globe also occupies a unique position in the newspaper world in the area. It does not belong to any combine, and it is not supported by the local big business interests. It started out as an

189

independent sheet in the bad old days just after World War I, and its earliest triumph was the exposure of the Big Joe Herschel set-up. This famous scandal achieved two things. It woke up the people of Monkton to a point where they would never again tolerate an administration so corrupt, and it established the Globe as a hard-hitting paper which would tell the truth, no matter who was concerned. The editor for the past eighteen years had been Shad Steiner, an old-style newspaper man who was popularly reported to have fifty per cent printer's ink in his veins. When I walked into his office, he nodded.

'Lo, Preston. Been a long time. I'm afraid I'm pretty busy right now.'

Shad's face was lined and worried. At fifty-three he was already old, but he'd looked exactly the same ever since I'd known him. It didn't mean a thing.

'Not just a friendly visit, Shad. Thought we might do a little trading.'

'Trading?' His eyebrows went up. 'I'm a poor man, Preston. What could I barter with?'

'Information,' I replied.

'Ah yes,' he nodded. 'Information. Now you're getting to me. I got practically all the information in the whole wide world. What I haven't got on the files I got up here.'

'Trouble is, Shad, I don't have a lot to offer,' I confessed. 'Except that you may get a nice fat story. Not an exclusive even, but at least you'll get it first and you'll have information the other sheets won't get.'

He frowned slightly.

'Preston, if we're going to do business, please remember this is the Monkton City Globe. Don't come in here calling my paper a sheet. Now then, what do you want to know?'

'Ever hear of a man named Swenson, Harry Swenson?'

'Sure, I heard of him. Next question?'

'I'm interested in a little murder we had yesterday. Guy by the name of Hudson was chilled.'

'The ice-pick thing? Swenson did that?'

I laughed.

'Come on, Shad, you know it can't be

as simple as that or I wouldn't be here. You also know another man was knocked off this morning. I saw two of your boys in the building where it happened.'

'I know it,' he confirmed. 'Another ice-pick. Is there any other connection?'

'I think so. I also think I'd get on a lot quicker if I knew more about Swenson.'

'I see. Pardon me if I seem rude, but what makes all of this any of your put-in?'

I could tell by his tone that Shad was interested. I also knew he was a man I could trust. Any newspaper man could have dug out Swenson's history for me, but the only one I cared to trust was Steiner. Which was why I went to him in the first place. I took a deep breath and told him some of the story. Not all. I left out Mrs. Whitton altogether, among other things. He listened carefully, without interrupting once.

'I heard about the saloon-keeper getting roughed up last night,' he informed me. 'Nothing for publication, naturally. The man didn't file a complaint, so officially nothing happened. And I don't like the part about the anonymous tip-off on friend Smirnoff.'

'Why?'

'No special reason,' he shrugged. 'Just don't like anonymous callers that's all. If you were a newspaper man you'd understand that. Anyway, leaving that aside, it could make a story. What makes you so interested in Swenson?'

'There's something going on,' I told him. 'I have an idea these killings are not personal things. Not the jealousy, hate, revenge type at all. I believe they're business killings, and the only man I've seen so far who even looks the right size for anything like that is Swenson.'

'Ah. You mean you don't necessarily suggest Swenson did the hard work himself, but you think he could be behind it?'

'That's about it.'

He closed his eyes and thought for a moment.

'Could be. From what I remember about the man, that part could be true. Let's go down to the morgue.'

I followed him out of the small office

193

and down into the basement, where forty years of news clippings were gathered in an intricate file system. We walked along the rows of steel until Shad reached the place he wanted.

'Let's see, about here I think.'

The first file was a wrong guess but he got it at the second attempt. The slim brown folder was marked 'Swenson, Harry'. Shad began at the back of the folder and began to read.

'Yes, this is what I was thinking of,' he told me, passing the papers over.

The folder was open at a clipping dated five years earlier. Swenson had been investigated in connection with charges of prostitution. The police had secured an indictment, but the case had been thrown out at the preliminary hearing. Insufficient evidence to justify the expense of a public trial. I flipped quickly through the rest of the clips. They were all connected with show business, and there were several shots of Swenson with some of the better known showgirls who were under contract to him. I even knew one or two of the names.

'What d'you think? Make any sense?' queried Shad.

I shook my head wearily.

'Not much help, I'm afraid. You'd hardly call one preliminary hearing a criminal record, huh?'

He shrugged.

'I guess not. Anything else you want to see?'

'No thanks.'

I chatted with him another few minutes, then left. Although I trusted Shad Steiner all the way, it would have been asking too much of any self-respecting newsman to sit on the kind of story I thought I had. At the very least he'd put a couple of his men on to preliminary enquiries and such, and a wrong move now by anyone could easily cause the whole thing to go sour.

I dropped into Sam's Bar for a glass of beer and a sandwich. It was cool in there and reasonably quiet, just the place for a little hard thinking. Steiner had asked a question back in his office which I now wanted to think over. What made all this any of my business? I'd been hired to find a missing girl. For once in my life I'd had practically no trouble. The girl turned up the same evening, the client was satisfied, and that ought to be that. The rest of the stuff was police business, not Preston business. What I ought to do was get down to headquarters and tell them what I knew. Or rather, what I thought I knew. Now was as good a time as any to think about what I'd found out.

Myron C. Hartley booked in the conventions. Monkton City is a convention town, and we probably accommodate a couple of hundred such sessions in a year. Everyone knows the kind of thing. They start out with printed itineraries of conferences and meetings, and usually wind up with a speech from the corporation president or who-have-you. For a lot of the delegates the whole deal boils down to one basic thing. A week away from responsibility and especially from Mrs. Delegate. I don't know anything about the finances of these week-long binges, but it didn't need a big brain to work out that they probably meant a spending potential around the two million dollar mark, if not more in a year. Two million is a lot of business, and Myron C. Hartley was helping to decide where it should be spent. That was one important fact. The next was that Hartley knew Harry Swenson. After that I went away from fact and on to supposition, but it was strong supposition. Swenson hired out girls, ostensibly to the entertainment business. But entertainment can take some weird forms, especially when you have ten or fifteen thousand middle-aged one-week bachelors to cater for. Swenson had been mixed up with prostitution a few years earlier. Any police officer will tell you that's one of the toughest rackets to break. The reasons are fairly obvious. You can't have a case without evidence, evidence means witnesses, and who is going to stand up in court and say he's done business with a prostitute? So if the police had had enough on Swenson to swing an indictment he must have been in it up to his neck, even though he didn't actually go to trial. He'd seen the light, opened up his entertainment agency and apparently gone legitimate. If I was guessing right, all Swenson had done was to go underground. Provide only better-class girls to the right functions, as well as operating a straightforward business. And what a recruitment centre he had. Any girl who went in looking for a break in the acting business could be assessed as a potential recruit for Swenson's other interest, his real business. Sylvia Le Fay had been a receptionist for Hartley but according to Rourke she'd previously been a showgirl and model. What she'd told me fitted in very well with my theory about the connection between Hartley and Swenson. If they thought she might take the lid off a two million dollar racket because the police suspected her of murder, it could be that her fears were well-founded. Nobody in that line of business would risk one loose tongue which could blow up the entire operation. Hudson was dead already, although I hadn't any evidence that he was mixed up with Swenson. Wait a minute, though. Hudson went to Mike, and Mike went to Hartley. Hudson died the same after-noon, Hartley the following morning.

This morning. So there was some kind of connection however remote. The point was, what happened now? Although it was all very interesting, it wasn't really any of my business, except for the side bet I had with Sylvia Le Fay and I didn't feel that called for me to go sticking out my neck. Not unless she got in any real trouble. No, I knew what was keeping me around. It was Juanita. The college boys. One and Two had led me to her, and they worked for Hartley. So she figured in this somewhere. Suddenly I thought I knew where. If any of my reasoning about the Swenson-Hartley combination was right, it could account for the condition Juanita was now in. Innocent but impetuous girl from the sticks, thinking she knew all the answers. It wouldn't be too difficult to recruit a girl like that into a call-girl set-up. That's how most of them start out anyway. So that was what made it my business. I had to go on with it until I knew where Juanita Morales figured, so I could be sure she'd get whatever protection was needed when the balloon went up. For I had little doubt that

Rourke and the rest of the squad at Homicide would be bound to uncover all kinds of things once they started asking questions about Hartley. His death may or may not have had anything to do with Swenson, but it was a bad day for Swenson all the same. I knew something about Rourke and his questions. If Swenson knew as much he ought to be packing his bags right now. I finished up the beer and left.

Swenson had an office on Fourth Avenue. Most of what passes for entertainment in my fair city takes place along a desirable boulevard named Conquest Street. Strippers, pose-queens, legit hoofers and canaries, all work in the hundred and one joints of varying shades of respectability on Conquest. Fourth runs crosswise to Conquest at the more respectable end, and here you can book any kind of entertainment from a dozen assorted agents. Swenson had part of the second floor in a mediumrental block. I took the elevator up. There was a large waiting room with a raven-haired beauty in charge. Several of the chairs were occupied, all by women. Some of them looked like aspiring hopefuls, some as if they'd been around a long time. They all looked at me with interest which died quickly when they found I wasn't anybody in their line of business.

I walked over to the desk.

'I want to see Mr. Swenson. The name is Preston.'

'Have you an appointment, Mr. Preston?' She was brisk.

'No, but tell him I'm here,' I replied.

She smiled sadly, and waved a graceful arm towards the waiting girls.

'I'm sorry,' she said. 'Mr. Swenson is already seeing someone, and all these people are before you.'

'Tell him I'm here, honey. And tell him I'm next. Or would you like me to go and tell him?'

I made as if to push through the wooden swing barrier and she jumped up quickly.

'Very well,' she flushed. 'I'll go and let Mr. Swenson know you're here. But it won't do any good.'

Ten seconds later she was back, closing

the door marked 'H. Swenson, Private'.

'I'm next,' I announced.

She nodded and sat down again.

'Mr. Swenson is just finishing. He shouldn't keep you more than a minute or two.'

One of the girls whispered to one of the others and they both stared at me in an unfriendly way. I leaned against the desk watching the brunette.

'Swenson can't be all he claims as a talent-spotter,' I said to her softly. 'Otherwise what are you doing running an office?'

She looked up in a resigned fashion.

'I'm disappointed, Mr. Preston. From you I would have expected something a little better, As it is you're the seventh man this week to tell me that.'

Swenson's door opened and a girl came out. She walked quickly through the barrier, flashing a smile at the receptionist and managing to exclude from it not only me but all the others present. She seemed to be pleased with the result of her talk with the great man.

'Now?' I queried.

'Now,' confirmed the brunette.

I passed through the little gate, opened Swenson's door and went inside. He was seated behind a vast stretch of walnut which looked to me as though no work of any kind had ever rested on its gleaming surface.

'Well, well,' he greeted. 'The eye. And please sit down.'

He said the last part quickly because I was already sitting in a wooden chair facing him.

'Nice layout,' I told him.

'I already know that,' he replied. 'Now if there's anything I can do for you will you get to the point as quickly as possible. There are people waiting.'

'I saw them. Matter of fact there is something I want. Like to have another few words with Juanita. Can you arrange it?'

He frowned slightly, then smiled.

'For a moment I thought this was a gag of some kind. But I'm with you now. I'm afraid you credit me with a better memory than I have, Preston. Over four hundred girls on my books. I don't pretend to remember half of them. Juanita, you say?'

He turned to a small card-index cabinet in tooled leather and opened a drawer.

'I'm afraid this will be quite a job unless you know the lady's other name.'

'Morales. Juanita Morales.'

He ran his fingers over the cards, stopping now and then to examine one more closely. Finally he shook his head.

'Sorry. Doesn't seem to be one of my girls. Where's she working?'

'She isn't working at all,' I informed him. 'You might say she's resting just now.'

'Well then,' he spread his hands, 'I'm afraid you've come to the wrong place.'

'Oh. Hartley sent me here. Said I'd have to ask you.'

He frowned again, just enough to look mystified.

'Hartley? Who is Hartley?'

'Myron C. Hartley, of the M. City Tourist Agency. You know him.'

I made that a flat statement.

'Oh, that one. Yes, yes, I think we have met.'

'I think so, too. You were with him last night.'

His eyes narrowed slightly, then he sat back in his chair, finger-tips resting lightly on the polished desk-top.

'What is all this about, Preston?'

The tone was different. Up till now he'd been the busy agent, willing to help if he could, otherwise would I please excuse him. Now I was talking to Swenson.

'I already told you, it's about Juanita Morales. I told Hartley I wanted to see her again, and he said I'd have to ask you.'

He drummed lightly with his fingers.

'He's mad. I never heard of her.'

'I see.'

I took out my Old Favourites, lit one and fanned smoke through my nostrils. Swenson watched this performance without comment.

'You know, Swenson, you oughtn't to feel too badly towards Hartley. Some people are built for this kind of work. People like you and me, we fit in. Hartley isn't cut out for it. When I asked him about Juanita, he told me to go fry my face. Then I got a little rough with him and he just couldn't stand it. But he did his best, Swenson. He really did.'

The agent sat quite still, staring at me with cold eyes.

'So you roughed him up, huh?'

'Not too much,' I assured him. 'Nothing that will show.'

'And when was all this supposed to happen?'

'This morning, early. Before you were out of bed.'

'You're a liar,' he spat.

'So I'm a liar. Ask him.'

Watching me, he thought it over. Then he leaned forward suddenly, snapping down a key on a small inter-office mike.

'Get me Mr. Hartley,' he grated. 'And hurry it up.'

I shook my head slowly.

'All right, what's up now? Afraid I'm going to call your bluff?'

'No use calling him,' I replied. 'He won't answer.'

'We'll see.'

We sat looking at each other busy with

our own thoughts. Finally the buzzer sounded. Swenson flicked down the key again.

'Well?'

The voice of the girl outside was shocked.

'Mr. Swenson, the police answered the call. Mr. Hartley's — dead.'

'He's what?' Swenson almost shouted.

'That's right, sir, that's what the officer told me.'

Swenson sat hunched over the little box. Then,

'Peggy, are you still there?'

'Yes, Mr. Swenson.'

'Did they ask who was calling?'

'Yes, sir. I told them you wanted Mr. Hartley and then they told me — you know.'

'Yes, I know.'

He broke the connection.

'You didn't know?' I asked him.

'How'd it happen?' he countered. 'And how did you know about it?'

I smiled widely.

'About Juanita. I'd like to see her this afternoon. Let's say three o'clock.'

'To hell with Juanita,' he roared. 'What happened to Hartley?'

'When I came in here I was hoping you'd tell me,' I said.

'Me? I don't know anything about it. Why should I? I don't have any connection with Hartley.'

'Too late for that, Swenson. You've got to face reality. Now Hartley's gone, the police are going to rake over his affairs. You don't think they won't find out what's been going on, do you?'

He tried to regain some control. When he answered, his voice was quieter.

'Going on? Why, just what has been going on?'

'The convention thing. It's all going to come out, within a couple of days at most. All about the parties and the girls, and who provided them. Naturally, the police will be able to get ahead a lot faster, now that you've established your connection with Hartley by calling his office.'

'Ah.' He expelled his breath in a sigh. 'You're a smart fella, Preston. Some day somebody's gonna wonder whether it's such a good idea to have a smart fella like you wandering around. Sticking your nose in other people's business. Somebody may get sick of you.'

'Maybe. But it won't be you, brother. You're dead in this town. Or any other town for a while. Come up to date, Swenson. The party's over. You're through.'

'Think so?'

He smiled thinly and sat back. From an inside pocket he removed a slim silver cigar-case. From it he extracted a slender brown tube, cut it carefully with a gadget he took from his pocket. Then he set fire to it, sucking in his cheeks deeply until the cigar was well alight. His mind was racing away the whole time as he took this new fact, the death of Hartley, and fitted it into some intricate pattern of thought. He didn't look at me until there was a half-inch of fine grey ash at the end of the glowing tube.

'You're right, Preston. It won't be me who does anything about you. You don't annoy me at all. You haven't got a thing and neither has the law. I run a legitimate business. The books are in that safe over there,' he waved to indicate a standard office safe against one wall. 'If the law walked in here right this minute they could go through my papers with infra-red lamps for all I care. There's nothing here.'

'Only a chump would keep anything in the office. Nobody thinks you're one of those, Swenson. But there's something somewhere. And the cops will find it.'

'They'll find nothing except plenty of evidence that I run a good clean agency. I may have hired out a few acts to Hartley some time or other. Can't remember every little thing. But that's all there is. And if any eager beaver with a badge starts trying to get too nasty with Harry Swenson, he'll find himself walking a pavement again in Harbour Street. A citizen has rights in this town.'

I tapped ash nonchalantly on the desk top. The look I got was enough to shrivel a tree.

'Decent citizens have rights,' I agreed. 'Those rights don't include threatening police officers with political kicks in the head.'

'I wouldn't know,' he said, in a bored tone. 'Too bad about Hartley. Now you can get out. I have people waiting.'

'What about Juanita Morales?'

'Never heard of her. Try next door. They supply kitchen help.'

I shrugged and got up. At the door I said,

'By the way, if you're counting on much help from Schultzie and Sylvia Le Fay — I wouldn't.'

He was looking puzzled as I closed the door and went out. To the girl with the black hair I said,

'From what I hear you're going to be out of a job very soon, Peggy. If you need any help finding another one, call me up.'

I placed the white visiting card on the blotter in front of her. I left her looking mystified, too.

10

I got to the Oyster's Cloister a little before three in the afternoon. Reuben Krantz was in his private office. He was seated at a small table covered with a cloth the kind of snowy white the soap advertisers dream of. On the cloth was a huge dish and in the dish was a mess of pigs knuckles. A schooner of beer stood at the side. Krantz worked a systematic shuttle between the knuckles and the beer.

'C'mon in, Preston. Siddown. You like this stuff?'

'Not too often,' I admitted. 'It's murder for the stomach.'

He grinned.

'You got troubles. You should have my stomach. Every day it kills me a little.'

'So why not eat a nice cheese on rye? Something that will rest a little easier?' I asked.

'Nah. Man has to have some pleasure.

212

Besides I got a system. Here it is three o'clock. By five I'll be real low. By seven I'll be spittin' angry. Just the mood I like to be in by the time the slobs start rolling in.'

The slobs were the new-style carriage-trade customers who paid for the knuckles, and the snowy tablecloth. Krantz clutched at his middle suddenly, face screwed up. Then he released a loud belch that made me thankful we were in a private room. A beaming smile came on to his lips.

'Wow. That's better. What can I do for you, anyhow?'

'Krantz, you've been in the club business a long time. I want to know something, and I don't want the word to get around that it's me asking the question.'

'So?'

'So I was here with Mrs. Floyd Whitton Junior last night. Before she got the fancy name she used to be a blues singer around the joints. Goes back about four years now. Remember?'

He nodded, patting at his mouth with a

napkin of impossible whiteness.

'I remember. So does everybody else in town. What's the question?'

'I want to know who her agent was. Who was the man who got the bookings?'

He studied his beer carefully, staring down into the amber depths.

'Have to watch the bottom,' he explained. 'Sometimes you get kind of a sediment down there. Bad for the stomach.'

I waited while he satisfied himself there was no sediment. Then he drained off the rest of the beer.

'I wouldn't imagine her agent has any claim on her these days,' he told me. 'You want to hire her out as a blues singer I should approach her direct.'

'Why so cagey?' I wanted to know. 'There's probably half-a-dozen other guys who could tell me.'

'So ask 'em,' he retorted. 'And don't forget what I told you last night. That Swenson knows some funny people.'

Then he winked and bent over the dish again.

'Thanks,' I said. 'One I owe you. I

better get along. If I don't pull something out of the bag by tonight Rourke's going to toss me in the can.'

Krantz shrugged.

'It doesn't frighten people any more. All that rehabilitation and stuff. I know plenty of guys who live better in there than they do outside. See you.'

I thanked him again and left.

With what I now knew added to what I suspected my next call was really decided for me. A few miles south of Monkton City there is a pine-covered hilltop. It was on these slopes, so the story goes, that the old-time Indian Chief War Horse held the simple ceremony of handing over the famous land grant to Bonanza Charlie, the old prospector who later befriended Floyd Whitton Senior. True or not, Whitton believed the tale strongly enough to have built what he called his hunting lodge on the side of the hill. In later years he had extended the original building until it was quite an imposing property, standing out with it's attractive yellow walls against the green of the hillside. It was here that his widow Louise had retreated after the great man's death.

I parked between the trim flower-beds and climbed out of the car. At the back of the house a ferocious barking started up. I judged there were at least three dogs joining in the chorus, and hoped that they were safely locked away. They didn't sound to me as if they were barking for joy. A man dressed in a sober black suit stood in the open door at the front of the house waiting for me to approach.

'Good afternoon,' I said. 'I'd like to see Mrs. Whitton Senior if it's at all possible.'

'Good afternoon, sir.' He decided on the 'sir' only after a careful look at me. For some reason it braced my ego. 'I'm afraid Mrs. Whitton does not receive in the afternoons.'

'I see. Well, I have to talk to somebody. Is there a companion or anyone like that?'

'There is Miss Cherry. She is Mrs. Whitton's confidential secretary.' He even sounded doubtful about bothering Miss Cherry with me.

I took out another card and handed it over.

'Give that to Miss Cherry, will you

please? And tell her I'm calling on intimate family business.'

'Very well, sir.' He turned, hesitated, then, 'If you would care to wait inside, sir.'

I followed him into the small hallway and he indicated a red leather chair. Then he slipped through a door and disappeared. I would have liked to smoke, but thought better of it. An elderly maiden lady like Miss Cherry would probably think it bad-mannered. After about five minutes the door opened again and the old man appeared.

'If you will step in here, sir, Miss Cherry will see you in a few moments.'

I went into a small room fitted out with fragile white painted furniture. To me it looked like hand-carved Spanish colonial, certainly too fragile for a man to sit on. I stood over by the fireplace studying a large portrait of Floyd Whitton Senior which had been painted in his prime. A tough old bird, the aggressive spikes of his brown moustaches fairly bristled from the canvas.

'Mr. Preston?'

A light voice from behind brought me quickly round. Miss Cherry was not yet due for that wheelchair I'd envisaged. A tall slender girl with deep chestnut hair combed out into soft waves. She wore a lemon sleeveless blouse and a flared green skirt. Her face was striking, not beautiful exactly, but with strong clean lines to it. From behind the thick black tortoiseshell glasses she surveyed me with mild interest.

'Miss Cherry?' I asked ridiculously.

'Yes. You said there was something about the family — ?'

She left the sentence unfinished and gave me to understand the word family began with a capital 'F'.

'Miss Cherry, please don't misunderstand this, but I don't really feel there's much to be gained by my talking to you. It's Mrs. Whitton herself I want to see.'

'I'm afraid that's out of the question,' she was totally impersonal. 'However, if you refuse to discuss it with me, perhaps I should show you out.'

I hadn't been to the trouble of coming

out in that afternoon sun to be brushed off by the help.

'Miss Cherry,' I said carefully, 'I'm not suggesting you don't know your own job. But in this case I think you may be assuming more authority than you have. When I say I'm here concerning trouble, trouble which involves the name of this family I am not exaggerating one little bit. Now, your approach is probably fine for newspaper reporters, salesmen and anybody else who mustn't be allowed too far past the dogs. But I don't come in that category.'

'You don't? Precisely what category do you visualise for yourself, Mr. Preston?'

If I was making any impression on this slim redhead she was contriving to conceal the fact.

'I'm an investigator,' I replied gently. 'It's on the card.'

She glanced at the small piece of pasteboard in her hand.

'Yes, so I noticed. It doesn't mention anything about why you've come to this house though.'

'No, it doesn't,' I agreed. 'But don't let

it bother you. You'll be able to read the whole thing. In large print, all over the front of every yellow rag on the coast. Unless we do something to prevent it.'

She smiled. Her teeth were small and regular, and very white.

'What a dramatic man you are, Mr. Preston. Last month we had a caller. He was very dramatic too. Wanted to protect Mrs. Whitton from radio-active fall out, For a price.'

'Ah, that's the pay-line,' I nodded. 'You don't have to worry about that angle. I don't want money and I don't want any favours. Just a few words with Mrs. Whitton.'

She tapped at the card with a thoughtful thumbnail. There was no varnish to spoil the slim brown hand.

'Supposing I went to Mrs. Whitton,' she began. 'I can tell you now that she'll refuse to see you. On the strength of what you've said so far, that is. Give me a little more. Just enough to make her want to hear the rest.'

'All right. Try organised prostitution. Then you could mention homicide.

That's another word for murder, Miss Cherry. Two murders so far.'

The shocked expression on her face was not assumed.

'You're seriously suggesting that I tell Mrs. Whitton her name might be associated with horrible crimes like those if she doesn't see you? You're mad.'

'No, I'm not mad. And I'm not necessarily saying that Mrs. Whitton's talking to me is going to make any difference. But at least she'll know what's going on.'

Miss Cherry started to speak, changed her mind, then turned and walked out of the room. She had long straight legs and a tight little behind that swayed in a most provocative way. Not that she impressed me as a girl who'd be pleased to have her attention drawn to it. I turned towards the portrait of old man Whitton, and I would have sworn he was grinning too. After all, I remembered, he didn't marry Louise until he was fifty-six, so he must have been all they said he was. While I was speculating about him I heard someone coming into the room. Louise

Whitton was another tall one, a handsome woman with elegantly styled white hair. Now in her sixties, it was still plain to see how an elderly confirmed bachelor like old Floyd had decided to marry her. She had bright piercing eyes, and there was nothing of old age in the voice.

'Young man, if you're wasting my time, I've given instructions that the dogs can have a turn at you when you leave the house. Now, what is all this rubbish?'

She sat herself down decisively in one of the flimsy-looking chairs. It didn't even squeak. Miss Cherry had followed her in and stood now by her side.

'Mrs. Whitton,' I began, 'I've already explained to Miss Cherry that I don't think you would want anyone else to hear what I've got to say.'

'Poppycock,' she snorted. 'This child knows everything that goes on around here. What I pay her for. Now then you, Mr. — er.'

'Preston,' supplied the redhead.

'Preston. Get on with it.'

She sat bolt upright in the chair as if ready to leave the house at a moment's notice. Two strings of flawless matched pearls hung around her throat, and on her left hand was an ornate silver ring mounted with the largest emerald I'd ever seen. She looked every inch what she was, one of the wealthiest and most influential women in the state.

'I'm an investigator — ' I started.

'What kind?' Then seeing my puzzlement. 'There's all kinds. Grubby little men stealing about hotels at night looking through keyholes. Semi-criminals, keeping information from the police if there's money in it. Honest men, doing work the police can't manage because they're overworked already. The last kind are mostly retired police officers. You don't look like one of those.'

I shook my head.

'No, I'm not. You only mentioned three kinds. If I have to be one of the three, I guess you'd call me a semi-criminal.'

She grinned broadly.

'Good. That's an impressive start. Tell me some more.'

'I've been retained by a man to find his daughter. She came to Monkton City and

223

took a job as a ladies maid. Then a month ago she walked out of the job and disappeared. The lady she was working for was your eldest son's wife.'

'Huh,' she trumpeted. 'That one. I had a feeling you'd mention her sooner or later. What'd she do? Poison the maid and hide the body under the garage?'

I smiled slightly.

'No. Sorry to disappoint you. Nothing like that. I went to see Mrs. Whitton Junior, find out what she knew about the missing girl. She couldn't tell me much, except that the girl was brought to her by a friend of hers. A man, by the name of Hudson.'

Miss Cherry uttered a small exclamation, and the old lady turned to her.

'What does that convey, exactly?'

Before the secretary could reply I got back into the story.

'I think I know, and I'm just coming to that part. I went to see the man Hudson. He didn't even remember where he met the girl, so I was back where I started. It was yesterday afternoon when I saw him. Through watching him, I was led to another man. Myron C. Hartley.'

'Sounds like one of these vaudeville acts,' interrupted Mrs. Whitton. 'You know, Hudson and Hartley, song and dance, bird imitations. Go on.'

'They have done a kind of double act, Mrs. Whitton,' I replied. 'An hour after I left him, Hudson was murdered. Then this morning Hartley was killed too. And in the same way.'

'Phew,' she made a face. 'You don't seem to be a very healthy young man to know, Mr. Preston. What has all this to do with my family?'

'Hartley,' I resumed, 'managed a tourist agency. It was a front for a much bigger business. He arranged most of the conventions we're always having here in Monkton. He'd see to hotels, banquets all the trimmings.'

'Thought you said the agency was a front?' she demanded. 'There's nothing illegal about booking hotels and so forth, is there?'

'No, ma'am, there isn't. But that wasn't quite all Hartley did. He also arranged — er — private entertainments for the conventioners. Very private entertainments. The girls were supplied by a semi-legitimate entertainment agency run by a man named Swenson. Swenson was the real boss, so far as I can make out.'

Her eyes sparkled.

'This'd make a hell of a good story for one of those tee vee crime things. Have the police arrested Swenson yet?'

I was beginning to find her enthusiasm bewildering. She was interested in the story as a story. Not as something which might drag her name across the front page. I began to wonder whether she was taking any of it seriously.

'Swenson was still free when I left him a couple of hours ago,' I told her.

'And what about your missing girl, any luck there?'

'Yes, I was lucky. I went around mentioning her name, and last night two men took me to see her. The men work for Hartley, or did.'

'Why'd she disappear?' pressed Mrs. Whitton.

'Family matter,' I lied. 'Nothing interesting there.'

Her eyes narrowed, and when she spoke she was less boisterous.

'You say a man hired you to find his daughter. You found her. Would you mind telling me just why all the rest of this, interesting though it is, should be any of your affair?'

I nodded unhappily.

'Two reasons really. For one thing, I've stumbled into all this by accident, but just the same I stumbled. So it's as much my business as anyone else's to assist the police when there's been a crime. Especially large-scale crime like the call-girl thing.'

'That's one reason. What's the other?'

'The police think I know a lot more about this than I really do. Having a private licence brings its own headaches. One of them is that policemen never believe you don't know more than you're telling. They know I called on Hudson just before he was murdered, therefore my visit must have a connection. Therefore, I'm holding out on them. And if I don't come up with something by tonight they're going to pick me up.'

'Arrest you? On what charge?' she asked.

'In a case of double murder almost any charge will do for a private operator. Suppressing evidence, collusion, anything at all.'

She nodded, the bright eyes never leaving my face.

'Well, you seem to have a problem young man. However, that's your business, not mine. If you've finished with all the background stuff, please get to the point that brought you here.'

Miss Cherry hadn't spoken since Mrs. Whitton arrived, other than to supply my name. But she'd been listening with absorbed fascination while the old lady and I talked. She too didn't take her eyes off me, and I was sure if I made a sudden movement she'd scream and jump out of the window.

'Mrs. Whitton, I'm fairly certain that if I go on with this I'm going to find some strong connection between your family and all the things I've been telling you up to now. Consider a few facts. I started out trying to trace a missing girl. Her last

228

known address was your son's house. She worked for your daughter-in-law. The man who got her the job was a friend of Mrs. Whitton Junior. Soon after he talked to me he was murdered. Last night Mrs. Whitton was drinking with two men. One of them was Hartley who was also murdered this morning. The other man was Swenson, who's been operating a major league call-girl racket. Before she married your son, Dixie Whitton was an entertainer. Her agent was Swenson. There are too many links, too many connections, to dismiss the whole thing as a string of coincidences. When I tried to put the squeeze on Harry Swenson a few hours ago he as good as told me he had big-name protection. We don't have a corrupt administration here in Monkton, but we do have kind of a royal family. Your family.'

She listened carefully, hands folded on her lap.

'I'd have to be naive to pretend I don't see any logic in your argument, Mr. Preston. But it still doesn't tell me why you're here.'

'I wanted you to know what was going on. Give you a chance to talk to your lawyers, take whatever steps you need to safeguard your interests.'

'Like hiring you, on a large retaining fee, to devote your attention to something less embarrassing?' she queried.

I sighed.

'No, ma'am, that wasn't in my mind. I already have a client who's paid me a hundred dollars to find his daughter.'

'A hundred? You're doing all this for a hundred dollars?'

The scepticism in her voice was edged. I began to lose my patience.

'What I'm doing it for is my own affair, Mrs. Whitton. The point is that I'm doing it. I'm going to carry on doing it. And I've tried to give you a friendly idea of the situation. Doesn't anybody ever come into this house who doesn't want anything?'

It was her turn to sigh.

'Not often. It is one of the things you come to expect when you're very wealthy. You're a strange young man, Mr. Preston. I have a feeling you also have leanings towards honesty. I appreciate your visit and what you've told me. Now go and do whatever you have to do. I shan't ask any favours for anyone in my family who is involved in the kind of thing you've been describing. If they think they can hide behind his name,' she pointed at the portrait of her late husband, 'they are mistaken. I bid you good afternoon, sir.'

She stood up, took a final piercing look at me and left the room. Miss Cherry waited to see what my reaction would be.

'She's a tough one,' I commented. 'Does she mean it?'

She nodded.

'She means it. There have been one or two attempts to get her to pay to have unfavourable news items suppressed. She always refuses.'

I looked round at the old man's picture.

'He knew what he was doing when he picked her,' I observed. 'She must have been almost as tough as himself.'

'They were well matched,' she confirmed. 'Tell me, Mr. Preston, do you really believe Dixie is mixed up in all this?'

I heaved my shoulders.

'Quien sabe? It all looks very complicated at the moment. But I've had a little experience on things like this. When you get something all jumbled up this way you suddenly find one little fact. Next thing you know everything looks very simple. Not complicated at all.'

'Well, I'm sure you're right. Shall we be seeing you again?' she ventured.

I looked at her. For a girl who had what she had, there ought to be more in life than playing watchdog for an elderly woman in a large lonely house.

'Maybe. You ever get into town?'

'Two or three times a week,' she replied. 'Mrs. Whitton is extremely generous about time off duty. This isn't one of those awful jobs you sometimes hear about where the poor little secretary lives in an attic with barred windows.'

'Good. Perhaps when you're coming in one day we could have a drink or something?'

'What kind of something?' she mocked

me with her eyes behind the tortoise-shell frames.

'That would depend on the circumstances. I'd buy the drinks and we could see what developed. O.K.?'

'Sounds fair enough,' she smiled. 'Call me in a few days, will you?'

I promised to do that, and left. Mrs. Whitton had evidently been satisfied with what I had to tell her. I didn't get attacked by any starving huskies on my way to the car.

11

I headed for Whitton Avenue and parked outside the Hotel Miami. For once I was in luck. The clerk behind the reception desk was the same man I'd seen the night before. He smiled pleasantly.

There was no recognition in his voice.

'I was here last night, remember? I called on Miss Morales in Suite 107.'

He managed to look sorry that he'd forgotten me.

'I'm sorry, sir. This is a large hotel and we have many visitors.'

'Of course,' I nodded. 'It doesn't matter whether you remember me. There were two young men with me. You knew them, because you told me so. Couple of overgrown campus kids, they work for Mr. Hartley. The conventions Mr. Hartley.'

'Ah yes, I do remember now, sir.'

He seemed so pleased with himself I decided he wasn't giving me an act.

'About Miss Morales, I guess she'll have checked out by this time?'

'Just one moment.'

He went to consult the leather and gold bound register. It didn't take him long.

'Yes, sir, the lady checked out at nine o'clock last night. No, she did not leave a forwarding address.'

He added the last part as he could see from my face what was coming. I stood thinking for a moment, then produced my licence. I always keep it in a flat leather cover, so that if I'm quick enough opening and closing it, the guy I'm showing it to might only have time to read the words 'State of California' in heavy official type at the top.

'I have to find the young lady.' I advised him, trying to talk in heavy official type. 'Those college guys can probably help. How do I get in touch with them?'

He was now an anxious citizen, eager to co-operate with what he thought were the authorities.

'That's very easy. They're in the hotel now.'

Seeing my surprise, he went on,

'We have a convention due into town tomorrow. Mr. Allison and Mr. Mount have been here most of the day, checking all the arrangements. I'll have them paged.'

His hand was halfway to the bell when I stopped him.

'No, don't do that. Like it to be a little surprise. Where do I find them?'

'Up on the second floor. There is a banqueting hall at the far end. They'll probably be checking the seating arrangements, or talking to some of the staff who'll be on duty tomorrow.'

'Thanks.'

I nodded to the clerk and went up the stairway to the second floor. The banqueting hall turned out to be a huge room, laid out for two or three hundred diners. At one end was a raised platform for speeches, cheerleaders and the cabaret acts. To one side stood the boys I'd come to see, deep in conversation with a French-looking man in a black tailcoat. At four in the afternoon. They didn't notice me until I spoke from a few feet away.

'Well, well,' I greeted. 'The all-Americans.'

All three whipped round, the waiter looked very puzzled. The other two exchanged glances. It was the tall red-haired boy, One, who spoke first.

'This is a pleasant surprise, Mr. Preston. We hadn't expected to be seeing you again quite so soon.'

'I'll bet. Where can we talk?'

'I'm afraid that's out of the question, Mr. Preston.' Two chimed in, the fat one. 'We have a pretty tight schedule for the rest of the day.'

'Ease it off,' I advised. 'We're gonna talk. Does he have to listen?' I jabbed a finger at the waiter who jumped as if I'd shot him.

'We're very pressed for time,' said One. 'But if you could make it fast, we can spare five minutes, Mr. Preston.'

He turned back to the waiter, asking him to squeeze in fourteen more chairs somewhere, then got back to me.

'There's a room over here at the side of the stage,' he led the way. 'Sometimes if we have a visiting speaker, he might like

237

somewhere to sit a while before he goes on.'

Two was beside me as One opened the door and stood aside.

'After you, boys,' I bowed. 'I have a superstition about being third into a strange room.'

They took me into a small room. There was a long seat running the length of one wall and a hi-fi cabinet. Otherwise the place was bare.

'Sit down fellers,' I advised.

Two looked as if he might argue, but One nudged him with his elbow and they sat down a few feet apart, legs stretched out across the soft grey carpeting.

'That's better. Which one is Allison?' I demanded.

'I'm Allison,' said Two, 'I wish you'd tell us what this is all about.'

'Sure. It's about the Morales girl. I'm going to have another talk with her.'

'Look, you talked with her last night,' snapped Mount. 'You heard what she had to say. What do you suppose you'll accomplish by dragging it all over again? Anyway it's impossible, she's left town.'

'I don't think so,' I informed him. 'Besides when we talked last night I didn't know what I know now.'

'Really?' asked Mount. 'And just exactly what is it that you know now?'

'Practically all of it,' I assured him. 'And what I don't know you guys are going to fill in.'

'C'mon, Pete,' Allison stood up. 'This man is wasting our time.'

I knew better than to try stopping these two husky characters all by myself in a room that size. Instead I took the .38 Police Special from my coat and waved it negligently towards them.

'Let's talk some more, you guys are growing on me.'

Allison would have ignored the gun, but Mount caught his arm.

'He means it.'

Reluctantly, they backed off and sat down again.

'This is preposterous — ' began Allison.

'Preposterous,' I rolled it round my tongue. 'I like it. It's a word that you don't pick up in the dime funnies. Tastes like a nice leisurely English major course, with hot rods and root beers on the side.'

Mount laughed shortly.

'Would you believe it? A snob. A snob hoodlum. Now I've seen it all.'

'Tell me about some of the things you've seen, Mount. Tell me about Hartley and Swenson, and the strip cabarets and stag comics. Tell me about the call-girls and the city hall protection. Stuff like that.'

'Except that you sound exactly like one of these crime commission characters on television, I don't know what the hell you're talking about,' replied Mount slowly.

'Must have worked out pretty good for a couple of well set-up young guys like you. Free booze, and plenty of spare tail around when some of the revellers got too drunk to care any more.'

I was trying to goad them. Allison flushed but said nothing.

'And now it's all over,' I clucked sadly. 'All in the past. But you don't have to worry. You'll probably pull a light sentence, one to four or thereabouts.

When you get out you'll still have your whole lives ahead of you.'

'What did we do precisely?' queried Mount. 'Leave our car in a no parking zone? Our employer isn't going to like you coming round here threatening people. Innocent people.'

'Zasso? Just who is your employer at the moment, Hartley?'

It had occurred to me down in the lobby that if Mount and Allison had been working in the hotel most of the day, there was an outside chance that they didn't know they were technically on the unemployed list. I tried another channel.

'Look, I haven't any argument with you guys. You're only fringe characters to me. I think it went like this. Hartley needed a couple of frontmen, guys who looked clean and fresh. Guys who could deal with hotel stuff, shake hands with the visiting firemen, kind of summer camp hosts with an extra plus. You were elected. You knew about the girls and the rest of it but that wasn't your side of things. Long as you didn't ask any questions you were able to think it was all good clean fun.

That way you didn't have to worry too much about who was breaking what laws. Stop me if I get off course.'

Mount glowered at me but his red-headed partner was interested.

'What're you leading up to, Preston?'

'This. That sob-sister version I just gave you, that's the kind of line you always thought you'd take if any of this ever came out in a courtroom. Could have worked, too. Still could if you start talking right now. Only it has to be right now, because you just ran out of time.'

'We did?'

Allison looked at Mount, who shrugged to indicate he didn't know what I was talking about.

'All I want is a few answers, and another talk to Juanita Morales. Otherwise I'm turning you both over to the law.'

Mount smiled. He really had a very pleasant face. The last man who smiled at me quite so disarmingly followed by kicking me in the groin. I was in hospital for days. I took a tighter grip on the .38. He said,

'So you'll turn us over to the police. First you have to have a charge. Even if you manage to think of one Mr. Hartley's lawyer will have us back on the street within an hour. You're nowhere, Preston.'

I shook my head and smiled back. My smile might not have competed with Mount's in the ordinary run, but today I had the better reason to use it.

'I've already thought of a charge. It's murder.'

'Murder?'

They both spoke at once, then looked at each other.

'Don't look surprised,' I scoffed. 'One of you probably did it, hoping the other one would supply the alibi.'

'About this murder we did,' queried Allison. 'Who did we kill?'

'I can see you guys are just apprentices,' I told them. 'The first thing about a professional killing, you have to know who the victim is. This time I'll tell you. It's your old buddy Hartley.'

'Hartley?' It was Mount who recovered first. 'You're crazy. He's not dead. Why, we were with him last night. Anyway who'd want to kill him?'

'Who knows? You maybe, or him. Both of you for all I know. As to whether he's dead, go call his office.'

Mount got to his feet, watching the gun warily.

'What about that?'

'I'll just keep it pointed at your little sister here till you get back. Oh, and Mount — '

'Well?'

'You have exactly five minutes. After that I give Allison to the cops and put you on the car radio. You wouldn't get a mile.'

'I'll be back.'

After he'd left Allison ran his finger round the inside of his shirt collar.

'Hot,' he offered.

'You think this is hot wait till you get in that gas chamber,' I told him.

'Very funny. You ought to go on the radio,' he scowled.

'Bet.' I looked at my strapwatch. 'In four minutes from now, that's just what I'll be doing.'

He glanced nervously at the chunky watch strapped prominently around his own wrist. I pushed an Old Favourite in my face and lit it. We didn't talk any more. Mount came back inside the deadline. One look at his face was enough for Allison. Mount walked across the room ignoring me, and sat down where he'd been before. He'd been the tough one, the one I wasn't getting to. Now he was ready to talk.

'Well what'd you find out, for Pete's sake?' Allison was jittery.

Without replying, Mount looked up at me slowly.

'Why would they think it was us?'

'Easy. He ran the show, or your end of it anyhow. You got paid out in nickels and dimes while Hartley raked off all the cream. You knew the business, knew it could be handled without him. So you figured you didn't need him any more. Ph'tt.'

He laughed, but it wasn't the confident sound he'd made earlier. This time there was a nervous twitch to it.

'You're crazy. You must think the police are very dumb. They'll be able to tell right away we're not that kind. One look at us, at our families, the people we know.'

I blew out smoke and watched it hang in front of me in the hot still air.

'Sure, the police aren't dumb. They'll take a good look. Specially at the people you know. Think about those people. Think about Swenson, a known prostitution organiser. Think about some of the muscle men who tag around after him. These are the people you know. Think the law boys will like 'em?'

Allison was beginning to sweat slightly. At the thought of Allison being grilled by the tough experts from Homicide I could feel almost sorry for him. Almost. Neither of them spoke.

'You remember what Confucius said? Or was it Walter Winchell? 'Man who lies down with dogs must expect to catch fleas'. You guys now have them. In the king-size pack.'

'Pete, what do you think?'

Allison turned to his now acknowledged leader, who ignored him.

'What exactly is on your mind, Preston?'

'Tell me about Juanita,' I replied.

'That was nothing at all. Hartley called us. Told us you were chasing around looking for this girl. We'd never even heard of her till yesterday. He told us she'd got herself into trouble after one of our — er — parties. We were to bring you here to meet her, pitch you the story about our rich friend and she would carry the ball from there.'

'So she doesn't really have any protection at all?'

He sighed and scratched at the back of his head.

'I didn't think any more about her. Hartley must have been seeing she was O.K. After all, he knew where to find her fast enough. And another thing, if she knew you were out to help her there was nothing to stop her telling you the truth was there? So she must have been getting money from somebody. Hartley or somebody.'

It sounded all right. Unless it wasn't that she was satisfied at all. Unless it was that she was plain scared to do anything but get rid of me the way she'd been told. I made a show of agreeing with Mount.

247

'And you haven't seen her since?'

'No.'

They broke together, but Allison took it solo from there

'But I know where she is.'

Even Mount looked surprised.

'You? How come?' he asked.

Allison fidgeted with his collar again.

'Well, I felt kind of sorry for her. You know. After Preston left last night I went back up to 107 and had a talk with her.'

'So that was where you got to?' said Mount.

'Yup. I offered to take her home, but she said she had her own car, and anyhow she only had to get over to Palmdale.'

I felt let down.

'Palmdale is quite a sizeable section,' I reminded him. 'Was that all she said?'

He nodded.

'That was all she said. Except that I took her down to her car. It was a foreign job, very fast. An Alfa-Romeo, all cream.'

'Very fancy,' I observed. 'But where does it get us?'

'I said to the parking attendant I wouldn't mind a car like that, and he said no, nor the address that went with it. Told me she lives at Sierra Blanca.'

That was very much better. The Sierra Blanca is a luxurious apartment building in Palmdale, a towering white structure.

'Good. I'll go see her after we've had our talk.'

'Wait a minute, Preston.'

Mount waved an arm at me, then leaned back crossing his legs.

'Hartley is dead. So we're kind of out of a job. We may become murder suspects. It's fairly certain the police will want to talk to us about — let's say — other matters. We are in all kinds of trouble, as the man says. So why should we do anything for you at all? Doesn't look as if much can help us. Seems to me it's time you put up your end.'

That was a quick recovery from the shock of learning about Hartley.

'All you get from me is advice. If I blow the whistle on you college cuties, and then tell what I know about you, you'll both wind up with a postgraduate course in San Quentin. Answer one or two questions and I'll be on my way.'

'Sure,' scoffed Mount. 'And call the police from downstairs instead of upstairs.'

'No,' I contradicted. 'If you guys knew a little more about the world you think you move in, you'd know I don't play like that.'

Allison was less sceptical than his sidekick.

'It sounds all right to me, Pete. Even if he double-crosses us, what can we lose?'

'Our heads, that's what,' snorted Mount. 'You think those guys, the big guys, are going to forgive and forget? If we talk to this character we may as well get measured for that slab right now.'

'If you're talking about Swenson,' I interjected. 'He's all washed up. Swenson is last year's hat.'

Mount bit at his lower lip and surveyed me carefully.

'You want us to believe that?'

'I don't care what you believe,' I assured him. 'What I'm saying is, the minute Hartley died, Swenson was washed up. The police lost a conviction against him once. They don't like to lose

250

and they have long memories. If you think you'll get any protection from Swenson try it. Five'll get you ten he'll say he never heard of you.'

Mount nodded unhappily.

'That's true enough. I already called him, right after I found out about Hartley just now. Wouldn't even talk to me on the telephone. Told his girl to say he didn't know anybody named Mount or Allison.'

I grinned.

'What'd you expect, once the going got rough? This isn't the ball team. Did you figure Swenson would rally round for the college yell? This is the outside, fellers. It's lonely out here, specially when the heat's on. And the heat is on full.'

'I won't tell you anything that puts anybody else in jail,' Mount said. 'Long as that's understood.'

'I'm not talking about jail, Mount. Jail is police business. I don't care if you have five per cent of every call-girl in the state. I'm talking about the gas-chamber. Who bumped off Gregg Hudson?'

'Hudson? The guy who was murdered yesterday?'

251

This time it was Allison who spoke.

'That one,' I confirmed.

'He wasn't anything to do with us,' asserted Mount. 'I never heard of the guy till he got famous.'

'Me neither,' confirmed Allison.

With two peachy-sweeties like these it was hard to tell whether it was the truth or not. I stared at their frank, open faces and learned nothing at all. I started to question them about other things, and the more we talked the more convinced I became that they were telling the truth. They didn't seem to know much about anything. The general picture was something they admitted knowing, but it was all very vague. On details they were hopeless. They worked for Hartley, but he dealt with anything that was even remotely crooked. They looked the other way and minded their own business. They'd been hired to do a job and look the part. Organisation men. As the organisation was more unorthodox than most, the pay-cheque was proportionately larger, and Mount and Allison had almost convinced themselves there was no harm in what they were doing. Of Swenson they knew nothing, except that when he was around it was clear where Hartley got his orders. They'd seen some tough-looking characters with Swenson but never had to mix with them. After about twenty minutes of useless questions I gave up.

'I'm going to take a chance on you two,' I told them. 'I promised no cops and that's the way it'll be. One thing, though. If I don't tell the law about you, and anybody finds out, I'll be in deep with the police department. So as from now, I never heard of you and you never heard of me. Understand?'

They nodded. I put the .38 back under my arm and went to the door.

'What'll you do anyway?'

Allison shrugged.

'What's it to you? We're strangers.'

I left them with plenty to talk about. It was now past five and I wanted to call in at the office before going over to Palmdale.

Florence Digby, for once, was not clacking at her typewriter. She had a large glossy magazine open on her desk and was flicking idly at the pages.

'Hallo, Miss Digby. Anything breaking around here?'

She gave me one of her disapproving looks.

'Mr. Preston, I only work here. Naturally I don't expect you to show up at the office very often, but it would be nice if a poor working girl had some idea of where you were.'

'Yeah,' I was shamefaced. 'Things got a little confused today what with the other murder and everything.'

That was enough to pique her curiosity. I had to spend five minutes filling her in on the murder.

'Now that you've gorged yourself on blood, how about telling me what's new with my business?'

She consulted the white pad that rests beside her telephone.

'That man Charlie something whose name I can't pronounce, he's called twice in the past hour. Seems very excited.'

She meant Charlie Surprise. His real name is some Italian name with about seven syllables to it which nobody ever could pronounce. Something like Supro-settomolino or what have you, which the linguists of the Harbour area had reduced to Surprise.

'What's he excited about?' I asked.

'Mostly about your not being here. He wants you to call this number.'

'O.K. Anything else?'

'Yes a man named Swinson or Swenson called. He wants you to call him too.'

'Thanks. I'll go into my own office. Let's start with Charlie.'

When he came on the line it was soon clear that Miss Digby had not exaggerated one small bit about Charlie's frame of mind.

'Preston? Wassa big idea, eh? You double-crossed me. I'll never give you another piece of information. Tell you something else, too, I'm gonna make it my personal business to see nobody else in this town ever talks to you either.'

So far I hadn't even said hallo.

'Is that you, Charlie?'

And that started him off again.

'You can bet it's me, who else? Why, how many other guys did you pull a fink stunt with today? Lemme tell you, Preston — '

'Later, Charlie.' I butted in firmly. 'You can tell me later. One thing at a time. First off, what am I supposed to have done?'

He snorted derisively.

'Huh. You ain't supposed to've done anything. What you did do was to put the fuzz on to Bice Smirnoff, is what.'

It was true. Not the way Charlie thought, but true just the same. When Charlie told me Bice's address I'd been intending to go round and have a few quiet words with him. That much and nothing else. Hartley was alive then, before the comedian with the ice-picks got to him. His death changed the picture, and my plans. I didn't have any reason to suppose Bice would know very much about any of this, but I thought it would give the police something to do if they picked him up. If he knew something, well and good. If not, there'd be no harm done. Either way, Swenson would feel the breath of the law, maybe not down his neck, but too close for comfort. Under the circumstances I felt entitled to give Charlie a false impression. Not exactly lie to him, but let him gather the wrong idea.

'Preston, you still there?'

'H'm,' I mumbled. 'Trying to gather my thoughts that's all. Look, Charlie, I gather the police have been to see Bice, and you think I sent 'em to that address you gave me?'

The words seemed to have a calming effect on him. He didn't sound so accusing when he spoke.

'You trying to say you didn't put the finger on the guy?'

'Charlie, I give you my solemn word I have not revealed that address to a living soul.'

'Your solemn word? Guess you're levelling then, huh?'

'I am levelling,' I assured him. 'Now let's start again. What exactly happened?'

He was full of apologies.

'Say I'm sorry, Preston. I mean it. Real sorry. I just naturally thought — '

'Forget it, Charlie. No hard feelings. Now, about what happened — ?'

'Sure. Well — ' there was a pause, and I could visualise him crouched over the receiver with that screwed-up expression that always indicates the internal agony of Charlie's thought-processes. ' — It was this afternoon. 'Bout one o'clock. All of a sudden this car pulls up outside Bice's pad. The bulls start pouring inside waving heaters at everybody. Bice is upstairs, you remember. Well, he musta heard the noise and all, because next thing you know Bice starts banging away with that damn' great .44 or whatever it is. One copper got hit in the leg and all the others get out of sight.'

Charlie stopped for a moment to chuckle.

'You're not old enough to remember the good days, Preston, but I've been told by eyewitnesses the whole thing was just how it used to be. The lawboys creep up the stairs and kick down Bice's door and everything, but Bice has gone. While they were busy getting out of sight he dived out the windows and got away.'

I made a whistling sound.

'So now we have a gunman loose in

town. How's the officer, the one who got shot. And who was it?'

'Aw, he's O.K. Just made a hole in the fleshy part. Name of Kenton. You know him?'

'No. What's the drumming on Bice?'

For a moment he was suspicious again.

'I don't know where he is, if that's what you mean.'

'You know that's not what I mean. I want to know why the police wanted the guy. That's one thing. It would also help me to know why everybody thinks Bice ought to carry on in this way.'

'Oh.' Another pause, while the involved machinery inside his head coped with this new problem. 'Everybody thinks this has to be murder. Bice finally made the big time. Even guys who've known him years can't understand what else would make him start up his own Pearl Harbour. You think it's maybe these ice-pick things?'

'Who knows? Anyway thanks for telling me about it.'

I confirmed with him our arrangements for taking old Morales back to the border that evening. After we'd finished, Miss

Digby got Swenson on the line. I let him wait a little before picking up the 'phone.

'Preston,' I announced.

'Listen,' he sounded guarded, not at all the big talker he'd been a few hours earlier. 'You want to talk to me about a deal?'

'What kind of deal?'

'Not on the 'phone. Look, you want the guy who's leaving samples of kitchenware around. Right?'

'What about it? You going to give yourself up?'

'Cut it out, Preston. This is serious. I may be able to give you a lead to this guy. Interested?'

If there was no catch I was definitely interested. Just the same, I didn't want to seem too eager.

'Perhaps.'

'Sure you are,' he asserted. 'You know the Round House? There's a private room upstairs. See you there in twenty minutes.'

'No. I have a call to make. I'll try to make it one hour from now.'

He almost shouted down the 'phone now.

'For the love of Mike, Preston, this is urgent.'

'To you, maybe. One hour.'

I hung up. Before I saw Swenson again I wanted that talk with Juanita Morales. I had a feeling she might tell me one or two things this time that would help me when I kept my date with Swenson. And I only had an hour.

12

The Sierra Blanca towered whitely towards the afternoon sky. I glanced quickly up as I walked from the car to the entrance. Maybe I thought I'd see Juanita Morales waving from a window, in which case I was disappointed. There was an elaborate glass and mahogany case against the inner entrance wall. This displayed the apartment numbers in permanent silver lettering. Next to the numerals were slots into which were slipped white cards with the name of the current tenant neatly typed. Tenants could come and go, said the case, but the apartments go on for ever. I ran my finger quickly down the columns until I found the one I was looking for.

Apartment 414 was easy to locate. It simply meant number fourteen on the fourth floor. I leaned lightly on the buzzer and waited. Within seconds the door opened. She was wearing a halter-neck red silk blouse, and tight black ballerina pants. Last night she'd looked ill, today she was radiant. The raven hair was pulled back into a tight bun, a smooth sheen reflecting from the immaculate surface. If I'd been expecting the glad hand I was entitled to change my opinion. She frowned quickly when she saw who it was.

'Señor Preston? But I have nothing to add to what I told you last night.'

I swear she would have shut the door on me there and then only my large foot somehow got in the way.

'Let's go inside and talk some more.'

I pushed past her into a tastefully laid-out room. A television set was battling against the strong light from the sun. I walked across and switched it off. She closed the door and came after me.

'What is this all about, señor? And why do you force your way into my home like this?'

There was a deep chair placed close by an open window. I dropped into it and sprawled comfortably.

'First decent rest I've had all day,' I told her.

She glowered at me and took a cigarette from a sandalwood box. The match flared after two or three impulsive stabs at the folder. Nobody asked whether I smoked.

'It doesn't matter, I have my own.'

To prove it I pulled an Old Favourite from a side pocket, lit it and leaned back.

'Well, well, he's certainly looking after you in style isn't he? Swell apartment, nice clothes. Why, you already look better than you did last night. Much better.'

'I do not understand,' she pouted sulkily.

'Sure you do. Last night you looked ill, today you're glowing with health. Last night your clothes weren't exactly Paris-style. Today you look like a model.'

'I can't stop you if you insist on sitting there making your cheap remarks, Señor Preston.'

'Cheap?' I tut-tutted. 'These are compliments, honey. Little Spanish flower blooms overnight. By the way there's one other small difference. Last night you were pregnant. Did you have an operation this morning?'

I pointed at her tight, flat stomach. She snarled at me but did not reply.

'Now,' I grinned cheerfully. 'Now we're going to have another little talk. Not like last time. The real thing, without the orchestra. Just the facts.'

'How did you find me?' she asked.

'Swenson told me where you'd be.'

'Liar. Harry would not do this.'

'Oh yes. Harry would do this, chiquita. Harry would do anything at all to keep out of that gas-chamber. And that's what this is all about, you know. Murder. Whether it's Harry's idea to let you take that last walk instead of him I really can't say.'

'That pig.'

She practically chewed at the cigarette. I tried to look unconcerned as I said.

'Let's get on with it, Isabella.'

Her head jerked round towards me, eyes like coals.

'You have my name wrong, señor. I am Juanita Morales.'

'No, honey. You're a good-looker and

you're from Punta Felipe, but that's the end of your resemblance to Juanita. You're Isabella Martinez, and I have two officers from the Immigration Bureau waiting downstairs for you right now.'

'Immi — ' her hand flew to her throat, and for a moment there was terror in her eyes. 'But, señor, please, I cannot go back to my village. You do not understand. I will go anywhere, anywhere you say. But this I cannot do. They would — '

As if realising suddenly that she was talking too much, she broke off sharply, and stared at the floor. Her full breasts rose and fell with her quick deep breathing.

'What would they do, Isabella?' When she didn't reply I went on. 'You don't mean the police down there, because you didn't do anything wrong before you left. Not criminal anyway. So you must mean the people of the village. I've been in Mexico a few times. I know what happens in these small communities. The people have an old-fashioned idea of justice sometimes. All fire and slaughter. Tell me what it is you've done that would turn them against you, Isabella. Tell me about Juanita.'

I suddenly barked out the last words, and she started nervously. Then she began walking up and down, pressing her hands together, and all the time the words tumbling from her scarlet lips.

'I did not do anything — not to her — not to Juanita. She was my friend. The other thing — it was an accident — nobody meant her any harm — accident — she fell. This man — he would not have hurt her — '

'What man?' I cut in.

'I do not know his name. They did not tell me — '

She was shaking violently now as though the room had become suddenly cold. I jumped up from the chair and caught her roughly by the shoulders shaking her.

'Snap out of it. Those guys aren't going to wait all day down there. We haven't much time. If you don't want to be taken back where you belong, better tell me the whole story and damned fast.'

She looked up at me, tears brimming in

267

the deep eyes. A look of fleeting hope lay in them.

'You will let me go? You will hide me from these men?'

'I might. If I get it all, and right now. I'll find a way to get you out of here without them seeing. Sit down there and get a grip on yourself and start talking.'

Her eagerness to co-operate was almost pathetic, but I steeled myself against pity. Too many people were already dead, and there was just a chance that if this girl talked, others might be saved.

She started talking, haltingly at first. Gradually she gained confidence, as I prompted her with questions and kept her moving on the facts.

Isabella Martinez had come to Monkton City in January, A few weeks before that she'd met some U.S. citizen who'd been passing through. He'd told her to come over the border and he'd fix her up with a job. So she waited her opportunity, then left home. When she arrived she'd telephoned the number this man had given her. It turned out to be the talent agency run by Swenson. He told her to call round and see him. No, he couldn't fix her with a regular job right off, but a friend was running a party and he needed an extra girl. All she had to do was be nice to the men at the party. Maybe one of them could give her a job. That was how she drifted into the elaborate call-girl set-up operated by Swenson. To do her justice, Isabella was not complaining. She'd very quickly seen what it was all about, and decided she'd like it. There was plenty of money, clothes, a decent place to live. Every night there was drinking, gaiety of a sort. It was all a long ride from a dusty village in Baja California. But, she felt a little homesick occasionally. Finally she got the bright idea of sending for her friend, Juanita Morales. Together they could have a fine time, and keep each other company as well. So she got word to Juanita about a month later, and soon her old friend arrived in town.

Isabella hedged a little at this point but it didn't take very many questions before it became clear that she hadn't told Juanita the hard part of the life. What she sold her on was the fun and the high living, and to Juanita the life seemed typical of what she'd been led to believe by reading the tattered copies of the glossy magazines which occasionally came her way back home. So when Isabella finally landed an assignment for her room-mate as an extra girl at a convention party, Juanita was delighted. The party was to be held at a large hotel, and the girls were to arrive at nine. When they got there things were beginning to warm up. A stripper had been hired and all the men were looking forward to it. All except one. There was a man named Compton, one of the senior executives on the convention. He'd taken a big shine to Juanita right away. Made a big play for her from the start. Swenson told Isabella to be sure her friend treated Mr. Compton right.

'Swenson said that?' I queried.

'Something like it,' she confirmed. 'Finally this man, he takes Juanita into a room at the side. Juanita will not do what he wants. There is an argument, a quarrel. Then Mr. Compton, he attack Juanita.'

Isabella dropped her voice a tone, and the words came in whispers.

'They were standing by the window. Suddenly Juanita loses her balance. She falls from the window. It is eighteen stories high, señor.'

I nodded grimly.

'So this man Compton killed her. Oh — ,' I held up a hand as she began to contradict me, ' — Maybe he didn't mean it, but she was dead just the same. Then what happened?'

She hesitated.

'You must understand, señor, what I am telling you now, is what I now know. At the time, I did not know anything bad had happened to Juanita.'

'All right. Tell me what happened after she died,' I replied.

'One of the men told Mr. Swenson. He went into the room, saw what had happened and then he sent for me. Told me he wanted me to look after this man Compton for a few days. You must believe it, señor, I did not know Juanita was dead.'

'Didn't you wonder where she was?'

'I wondered. But Mr. Swenson, he said I was only to do as he tol' me. Otherwise I might get my face kicked in.'

She went on with details about how she took Compton to Swenson's apartment at West Shore. I didn't tell her I'd been to 24 Bahia Apartments the same morning. After a few days Compton was fit to go home. Swenson had been to see him twice a day. At these times he would send Isabella out, and presumably spent his time alternately cajoling and threatening Compton into a suitable frame of mind. When Compton finally left, Swenson sent for Isabella. By this time she'd gathered from Compton that something had happened to Juanita, but he wouldn't tell her any details. Swenson was a little more helpful. Juanita was dead. To him it could mean trouble. He wanted to know all about her, where she came from, who her family were, everything. When he was satisfied Isabella had told him all she knew he made her a proposition. Juanita didn't know anybody much so far, now she was dead. It would suit Swenson better if she didn't die for a while longer. Isabella was to take a job under Juanita's name for a few months. At the end of that she could leave the job, and as Juanita Morales, disappear. Isabella could then come back into circulation plus a fat bonus from Swenson for her trouble, and nobody would ever give Juanita another thought. Nobody except her family, that is. And Swenson could scarcely be expected to foresee that the family would hire somebody like one Mark Preston to start nosing around.

'So you got the job at Mrs. Whitton's home,' I mused. 'How'd you come to land that?'

'Mr. Swenson arranged everything. He tol' me Mr. Hudson had a friend who had the job for me.'

'Hudson?' I queried.

'Si. He used to work for Mr. Swenson sometimes. Sometimes he make a little pass at Isabella, too. I knew him. It was the same Mr. Hudson who was killed yesterday.'

'I wondered if it might be,' I admitted. 'So you worked for Mrs. Whitton. Then, a month ago Swenson said it was time for you to leave. Right?'

'Si,' she nodded. 'Then yesterday he telephone me. Some man, you señor, was looking for Juanita. He was arranging for me to meet the man last night. The rest you know.'

Whatever I was thinking as I looked at Isabella standing there I couldn't quite analyse. What kind of girl will let somebody cover up the murder of her friend, then go to a lot of trouble to make the cover good? I knew the answer to that one, too. Principles that seem so clear and obvious in ordinary conversation don't stand out so vividly when you're a lonely girl in a strange country, with violent men waiting and willing to plant their feet in your face. For the moralists I have a sixty-four dollar question. Have you been there? If the answer is no, then clam up.

'Ever hear of a man named Hartley?' I asked her.

'Ah yes. Señor Hartley was also at the party. At all the parties.'

'Anybody else? Other men, I mean.'

She thought about it. She knew the college boys but not well. When I tried her with the names I got no response, but as soon as I described them she was with me. Hudson, it seemed was at the parties on some occasions, but didn't seem to be a regular member of the organisation.

'About Hudson, did he ever come out to the Whitton house while you were there?'

'Two, three times. 'Bout once a month, I guess.'

'Why did he come? Did he know the family?'

'Not Mr. Whitton. Mr. Whitton don' come home too much. I don' think Mr. Hudson ever saw Mr. Whitton. Always my mistress.'

I smiled encouragingly.

'They must have been pretty good friends, huh? I mean, he got you the job there, didn't he?'

She shook her head violently.

'Friends, señor? Sure, he get the job for me, but they were not friends. Whenever he come, they fight. Always they shout at each other. After Mr. Hudson leaves, my mistress always has a bad temper.'

'You think she killed him, Isabella?'

'Kill? Oh no, not Mrs. Whitton. Fight, yes. Use bad language, throw things at people. Sometimes even at me. But not kill.'

I checked my watch. If I was going to keep my date with Swenson I couldn't spend much more time with Isabella.

'About last night,' I said. 'After you finished selling me the gold brick, what did you do?'

'I came home. Came here. Mr. Swenson wanted me to report to him how my talk with you went.'

'Swenson came here?'

'Oh yes. He has a key. Mr. Swenson has a key to all the apartments of girls who work for him. He says he likes to know what is going on.'

I frowned.

'All right, he was here. What happened?'

Isabella sat down suddenly, close by the now-still television.

'He was very excited. Wanted to know

every word you said, every answer I gave you. He was here over half an hour. All the time questions.'

'Excited? How do you mean, exactly?'

'It is hard to describe, señor. He was upset, you know. Waved his arms, shouted at me, that kind of thing. After I told him about our talk he was much better.'

I made a face.

'You mean after you told him how you'd suckered me into forgetting about Juanita Morales.'

Spots of dark red suffused her cheeks.

'Talk is very cheap, Mr. Preston. I am a call-girl in this town. That's the nicest description I would get from anybody. There are others, not so nice. A girl like me does as she is told, or else something happens to her. Something bad. And if it does, there is no-one to care. Whatever we get we asked for it. That is the view of the public. Did you ever hear of a blind call-girl, Mr. Preston? Or one with acid burns on her face? I do as I am told, and I stay healthy.' She spoke rapidly, but very distinctly. Isabella had had plenty of time to work out where she stood, and I couldn't argue with her. She was mostly right, from her slanted point of view. She went on. 'All right if you wish, I deceived you rather well, I thought. Mr. Swenson thought so, too. He gave me a hundred dollars and told me to keep out of sight for a few days.'

I laughed shortly.

'Something amuses you?'

'Ah, it's nothing. The whole things cancels out that's all. Juanita's father gave me a hundred dollars to find his daughter. Swenson gave you a hundred to supply one.'

She didn't think it was very funny. It wasn't. We talked to another few minutes but I didn't learn anything. When I said I was leaving she got very agitated. Wanted to know what I was going to do about the two imaginary immigration men downstairs. I'd forgotten them, but she hadn't. I promised to tell them we'd got the wrong girl and lead them somewhere else. That seemed to satisfy her. At six-thirty I was in the middle of a traffic crawl headed for the Round House.

13

The Round House is more octagonal
than round, but you couldn't call a bar
the Octagonal House. It's used a lot by
the business crowd, and has a number of
private rooms where the smart operators
can make a big impression on the
out-of-town buyers. Downstairs I asked
which room Swenson had hired. The man
said number six and I went up the narrow
stairway. When I passed room number
four a large man in a tight green suit rose
from a chair and got in my way.

'You're going where, mister?'

'Number Six. I have an appointment
with Mr. Swenson. You the butler?'

He nodded heavily.

'Little of everything. You know how it
is. Got anything heavy in your pockets?'

'Only a .38 Police Special, if you count
that,' I told him.

'I count it,' he said. Suddenly there was
a gun in his hand.

'Turn around and lift the arms way up.'

I did exactly that. He patted around until he found the gun, grunted, took it out of my shoulder holster.

'You can turn around again. What's your name, mister?'

I came round to face him.

'Preston,' I told him. 'Mark Preston.'

'Good, good. That's what it's supposed to be. Boss'll see you now.'

He motioned me past him and towards room six. I opened the door and went in. There was a table set for a meal. Four places were laid, but I had a feeling we weren't going to do any eating. Swenson sat in a wooden chair facing the door. He had a gun, too, a Luger this time. Some of the anxiety went off his face when he saw me, and he stuck the weapon back in the waistband of his pants.

'Expecting anybody else?' I asked.

'Maybe. Come inside and shut that door.'

I went further into the room and sat down at the table. The silverware was gleaming in the evening sunlight. I took a piece of celery from a dish where the ice cubes were beginning to dissolve.

'You want to see me, remember?'

I scrunched noisily at the celery. Swenson jumped irritably.

'Just left a friend of yours,' I told him. 'Isabella.'

His mouth twitched.

'Isabella? Who's that?'

'Not who's that, Swenson. Bad grammar. Who's she, you mean. And anyway you know who she is. She's the dame you put me on to last night. Only last night she had another name, and her figure was fuller.'

'So what?' he snapped. 'She didn't do you any harm.'

'True, true. Still, somebody did the real Juanita some harm, didn't they. Was it you, Swenson? That what this is all about? You killed Juanita, now you're having to kill everybody else in town to cover it up?'

'Crazy,' he muttered. 'You must be crazy. If you really think I knocked off those guys, and then you walk right in here unarmed, you must be off your head.'

I took another large bite at the celery

and waved the stick at him.

'You win. I don't think you killed them. Crazy I may be, but not so dumb that I'd walk in here if I thought that. Anyway, don't let's talk about me all the time. Let's talk about you. And why you want me in such a hurry, and why all the artillery and who else are we expecting?'

He tapped his fingers against the butt of the Luger. It seemed to give him reassurance, and judging by his face reassurance was something he could use.

'You don't know? We're waiting for Smirnoff.'

'Bice? Why?'

'Because he says he's going to kill me, that's why.'

I looked more interested.

'Why would he want to do that?'

'The guy's crazy. After Hartley killed Hudson he — '

'Whoa, whoa,' I held up a hand in protest. 'Little too fast. First let's hear about that. You say Hartley killed Gregg Hudson?'

He looked surprised.

'Sure. I thought you would've figured

that. After you talked to Hudson he sent a message to Hartley. Hudson wanted to blow town and he needed a stake. Hartley didn't take it very seriously until you showed up at his office too. Then he thought he ought to do something about Hudson. There was one man who'd talk his head off if he thought the cops might give him a bad time. So Hartley took a ride down there and knocked off Hudson.'

I took another crack at the celery.

'Well, well,' I observed. 'That about closes the file doesn't it? After he got rid of Hudson, Hartley spent a sleepless night crying on his pillow. Then he walked down to his office this morning, couldn't take any more. So he just committed suicide. Stuck this ice-pick in his back and that's the end of it.'

Swenson scowled.

'Very witty. No, this is where Smirnoff decided to get smart. You can't guard against guys like that. You build up a business, put in a lot of work, and it only takes a punk like that to blow up the whole deal.'

A cool breeze wafted in from the open window. I shifted slightly in the chair to take better advantage of it.

'What did Smirnoff do?'

'I've been having trouble with Hartley over one or two things. Him getting rid of Hudson like that made me real sore. We had a row. I told him it was the damn stupidest thing I ever heard of, and we all stood to wind up in the pen. I lost my temper, I guess. We called each other a few names. Then I got nasty. I told him to watch what he did for a while or Hudson might have company in the morgue.'

'And Smirnoff heard you?'

Swenson heaved his shoulders glumly.

'Yeah. In his stupid head he figured I wanted Hartley out and he could do everybody a big favour by killing him.'

'Will no-one rid me of this troublous priest,' I muttered to myself.

'Huh, what's that?'

'Nothing. So Bice thought he'd get himself a promotion.'

'Something like that. He even used an ice-pick, figuring the cops would connect Hartley's death with Hudson. That way

Smirnoff would be in the clear. He had an alibi a yard wide for the time of Hudson's death.'

There was a movement in the passage outside. Swenson stopped talking and his hand closed over the grip of the Luger. I watched the door nervously. If there was going to be a war I was elected as unarmed civilian and I didn't like it too well. Then the footsteps proceeded past and we relaxed. I said,

'So now Smirnoff wants to kill you? I don't think I follow that. If you want a promotion you don't knock off the guy who's going to give it to you.'

Swenson uncurled his fingers from the gun butt.

'After he got rid of Hartley, Bice came to tell me the big news. He looked like the cat that swallowed the canary. I told that pig to get out of my sight and stay away. Then this afternoon the cops tried to pick him up. There was some shooting and he got away. He called me up, thought I'd tipped off the law about Hartley. Said he was going to get me before the cops got him. I told him to cool off. Said I'd meet him here tonight and give him some dough to help him stay out of sight for a while.'

I thought about it.

'And this is your idea of a pay-off?' I pointed to the fat Luger. 'He walks in here and you blow his head off.'

'No. You're wrong. If he comes in and listens to reason he can have the dough.'

Swenson flicked his thumb towards a large envelope that lay on a chair.

'There's enough in there to take him any place he wants, and an extra grand for expenses. That's if he comes to talk. If he starts shooting, I start first. And I know he'll shoot, because he already told a friend of mine.'

'O.K.,' I nodded. 'So what am I doing here? You don't need me.'

'You're here because I think you're on the level,' he said. 'You're the only one mixed in this that the cops will listen to. If Smirnoff dies here you'll be able to say I shot him in self-defence.'

'I will? If I'm going to say that, it's going to have to be true.'

'It'll be true,' he assured me softly.

I started playing with one of the silver handled knives on the table.

'So where does that get you?' I queried. 'There's still the murder of Juanita Morales.'

'There is? Never heard of her. You show me a body by that name, and then I'll start to worry.'

He said it with complete assurance, and I was certain he was justified. If the girl's body hadn't turned up in all these months, there was no reason why it should be found now. Even if it were, identification would be a remote possibility. South of the border they don't have these medical case histories, dental records and so on that the police make such good use of for purposes of identification.

'Did Sylvia Le Fay know all this?' I asked.

'Sylvia?' he snorted. 'You think I'd trust a dame like that with this kind of material?'

'No,' I admitted. 'Sylvia's kind of worried. Thought you might think she killed Hudson. She used to live with him once.'

'I know that.' He chewed on his lower lip, then nodded. 'Yeah, I can see that. See what she means. I might figure she knew more than she should. She can quit worrying.'

'I'll tell her,' I promised.

He might have been going to ask what connection I had with Sylvia, but a voice suddenly grated,

'Swenson.'

It came from the window. We both automatically swung in that direction. Smirnoff was framed in the open space crouching like an ugly fat beetle. Like a toy in his great hairy hand, the blue .44 spat once, twice. The roar was deafening in the confined space. Swenson was already half way out of the chair, clawing the Luger free of his pants. The first slug hit him in the left arm but the second was on target, tearing an ugly black gap in his stomach. The deep red welled out around the hole and he screamed with the sudden agony of it. Gripping the chair with his damaged hand he fought to raise the Luger. Slowly the wavering gun came up towards the man squatting in the window. Smirnoff laughed, a gritty evil sound.

'Surprised, huh? She told me this was a set-up.'

The Luger was almost in position now. Smirnoff laughed again.

'So long, sucker.'

The big .44 kicked again, smashing into Swenson's chest. He fell backwards, clutching automatically at the Luger, which fired a harmless shot into the ceiling. I stood watching helplessly as Swenson's body crashed to the floor. Then the door burst suddenly open and the big man from the passage rushed in, gun in hand. He saw Smirnoff at once and shot without hesitation. Smirnoff had been taken by surprise as much as I had. The slug hit him in the shoulder. He shouted with pain as the heavy bullet spun him round on the narrow ledge. He tried to stand, grasping desperately for the frame of the window. His searching fingers scrabbled at the glass for a tense fraction of a second. Then with a scream of baffled rage and pain he plunged heavily down. I rushed across and looked out into the street, just in time to see him hit the concrete. The sickening thud carried quite clearly upwards, and he lay in the roadway without moving. Cars began to brake, one or two women screamed, and an excited crowd gathered round.

Back in the room the big bodyguard was kneeling beside the shattered remains of Harry Swenson. The gun was still in his hand and he looked at me uncertainly.

'Forget it,' I said quickly. 'You've got nothing to fear here. I'm your witness. You shot Smirnoff after he'd already killed Swenson. I was next, so you didn't have any choice.

He nodded.

'I guess so. Won't do me any good to blow.'

'Waste of time,' I assured him. 'If you really want to sew this up tight you'll step outside right now and call the cops yourself. Call homicide and get Lieutenant Rourke. He's a square guy and he'll see to it these precinct boys don't try to bear down on you.'

He got up, took a final look at

Swenson, then nodded again. Reaching inside his coat he took out my .38 and handed it across.

'We'll just forget I ever took this away from you, Preston. Bet?'

'Right.'

I shot out the clip and stuck it in a side pocket. Then I pushed the .38 under my arm.

'What you do that for?' he queried.

'Couldn't use it,' I explained. 'Don't load unless I'm expecting trouble.'

He grinned quickly.

'You think fast. Guess I will call the cops.'

He left the room. I went quickly to the chair with the envelope on it. Inside there was eighteen hundred dollars, in fifties and hundreds. It belonged to Swenson, only Swenson was dead. He didn't have any wife and family. Neither did I, but I was still alive. I slipped the money inside my jacket, and helped myself to a much-needed Old Favourite.

Soon there would be Rourke to deal with.

14

It was nine thirty as I walked out of police headquarters and down the worn stone steps. At the bottom I paused to take in a breath of the cool night air. It made a welcome change from a certain stuffy room up on the third floor. By his standards Rourke had been easy on me, but I'd been in that room the greater part of two and a half hours just the same. Rourke was feeling almost human when I left. We were practically friends again. From where he sat it had been a good day. In a little over twenty-four hours he'd had three homicides and a self-defence killing. All those responsible for the homicides were dead, and there was a large man in a detention-cell on the manslaughter rap. I'd maintained my stand that I'd become involved by accident. Making enquiries for my client Mrs. Whitton on another matter, I just stumbled into this thing and it was none of my business. I didn't know why Hartley killed Hudson, and I only had Swenson's word for it that he had. It could have been money, or a woman or anything. With Hartley himself now among the departed it was doubtful whether we ever would know. In any case, did it matter too much? There was this vice organisation, now shattered. As a bonus the department should accept it with gratitude, and not go poking around at every little fact that wasn't fully explained.

Rourke wasn't really out to make trouble for me, I knew that. All he was interested in was getting crime files sent to the 'solved' section. Tonight he would be able to mark up a good score before he went to bed. Now he was through with me, and there were just one or two little things I had to do before I bought myself a well-earned drink. A girl walked slowly along towards me. She wore a black peasant blouse and a tight white linen skirt. Her heels must have been clear of the ground by seven inches as she teetered along on those wicked-looking spikes. When she got close the glow from a neon street light picked out vividly the naked lines on her hardening face.

'Hello, handsome,' she began. 'Did you want — ?'

I turned and walked quickly away. She whispered a word at me. The voice was soft and penetrating, the word harsh and equally penetrating. There was a cab rank at the corner of the block. I flagged one and told the driver where to take me. My own car was still parked outside the Round House, since the police insisted on providing transport to headquarters for me after the shooting. In the back of the cab I took the empty .38 from its holster, slipped the cartridge clip from my coat and slid it into position. There was a smooth click as I rammed it home with the heel of my hand. I heard a gasp and saw in the overhead front mirror the wide-eyed face of the cab-driver. I chuckled.

'It's all right, friend. I have a licence for the thing.'

To set his mind at rest I shoved it back under my arm and then he relaxed sufficiently to watch the road. Just the same he kept half an eye on me all the rest of the way. He was clearly relieved when I climbed out and paid him off. I went straight up this time and pushed at the buzzer with my forefinger.

Isabella opened the door. She wore the same outfit I'd seen earlier. She grinned at me foolishly.

'Hah. The big detective. Come in señor, I pray.'

I went in. There seemed to be a party going on. A half-empty gin bottle stood on a side table. There were two glasses, each with some drink still standing. A box of potato chips had tipped over, and a spray of the crinkly chips had fanned out over a rug. The hi-fi was grinding out some loud brassy music. Isabella put one palm on her tight stomach and danced around, singing. There was no-one else on view.

'Are we celebrating something?' I asked.

When she made no answer I walked across and turned the volume down. Then I repeated the question. She nodded and smiled.

'You take a drink, Mr. Preston?'

She went to the gin and would have poured some for me.

'No thanks, I never touch it. Why gin, anyhow? Couldn't you raise any tequila?'

Walking up to me she ran her hands up the lapels of my jacket.

'My big detective,' she murmured. 'I could really go for a man like you, señor.'

She was slightly drunk, and the liquor put fire in her eyes and animation into her body. Isabella Martinez was a whole lot of animal woman and I knew if I didn't watch it I could easily like the idea of her being close to me. Very close. I picked up one of the half-full glasses and put it into her hand.

'Where's your friend?' I queried, pointing to the other glass.

She smiled oddly, and tossed the gin down her throat. She drank quickly and without seeming to swallow at all.

'Why are you here, señor?'

'Wanted to tell you what happened tonight. To your friend Harry Swenson.'

She pouted.

'Phui. I heard. There was a news item on the radio. Poor Harry.'

'Yeah,' I agreed. 'Poor Harry. I knew you'd be all cut-up about it.'

She laughed then, a deep throaty chuckle, tilting her head back to enjoy it.

'I've been with the police all evening,' I went on. 'They asked me lots of questions, Isabella. Nasty questions, some of them. But you don't have to worry, honey. I didn't tell them it was you killed Swenson and Bice Smirnoff.'

Her face darkened momentarily.

'I? Not I, señor. It was all on the radio. Besides, I was right here in this room the whole time. Ever since you left.'

I nodded, walked across and sat down in a chair close by the door. She watched me with the hooded concentration of someone who'd had too much to drink, but still wanted to watch what she said.

'I know you weren't there, angel. I was right with Swenson when it all happened. I'm prepared to go in the witness stand and swear you weren't there. But you killed him just the same. Smirnoff too.'

She took another splash at the bottle

and stood facing me, glass in hand.

'Crazy,' she accused. 'You're crazy, Mr. Preston.'

'Uh, uh,' I denied. 'Swenson told me Bice had arranged to meet him. Wanted some money to clear out. Swenson said he didn't believe Bice. Thought he was really coming to the Round House to kill him.'

'So,' she shrugged. 'That was true wasn't it? Unless the radio had it all wrong.'

'No, the radio was right. What the radio didn't know, and neither does anybody else but you and I, was that somebody told Smirnoff Harry would kill him as soon as he walked in the door. That was you, honey. You told them both.'

Isabella stared at me, tapping with one foot at the grey rug.

'I did that? You can prove it?'

'No,' I confessed. 'And I don't know it would matter very much if I could. In the eyes of the law I doubt whether you've actually committed any crime.'

'Then it does not matter, huh, señor?'

I shook my head.

'Not to anybody but us. Why? That's all I want to know from you. Just tell me what those guys had done to you that would make you act that way.'

'Have you a cigarette?' she asked abruptly.

I broke out a couple and lit them. Isabella went and sat down on a day couch affair. Leaning her head back against the gold cushions she released a cloud of smoke and watched it spiral towards the ceiling. Then she spoke.

'I have decided. I will tell you, Señor Preston. After all, I owe you many thanks for what you have done. Without you I do not think it would have worked half so well.'

I inclined my head in acknowledgement but said nothing.

'You ask what these men have done to me. I answer you, almost nothing. They once say they will kick me in the face if I do not do as I am told, but this is nothing. It is only talk. I have heard much such talk in my life. None of it ever hurt me.'

She flicked at the end of her cigarette

with a thumbnail and a fine spray of ash fluttered towards the floor.

'We must go back, señor. Back to the night they murdered my beautiful Juanita.'

'I thought it was a stranger, a man named Compton, who did that,' I interjected.

'Pah,' she spat. 'Compton was just a drunken pig. Certainly it was he who cause her to fall. But his was not the real blame. He thought she was just a whore, he was not to know she really meant to resist him. It was the others, Swenson and the other animals. It was they who gave her to him.'

I looked around for an ashtray, found none, finally dropped my ash on the floor, too.

'But she was there,' I pointed out. 'It wasn't exactly a graduation party from a finishing school, was it?'

'No,' she said softly. 'I will tell you how it was, señor. When I sent for Juanita to come here to join me, I did not mean her to live as I lived. She could share my home, but I would have found her a job, a

300

proper job. Then the great Mr. Swenson walked in one day and saw her. He told her she was very beautiful. Said I ought not to keep her from having a good time. He asked her to the party and he knew I would not dare to stop her. Not that I could. She was a child, señor. Juanita was not really wild, like me. There was no badness in her. Perhaps that is why I loved her so much.'

Isabella fell silent for a moment. It was no time for me to be talking, so I sat quite still and waited.

'After — after it happened, Swenson sent for me. I told you before what he said. I didn't tell you what they did, those dogs, with her body.' There was a catch in her voice. 'They took that poor broken body out to the city dump, señor. They covered her with the garbage of this rotten city and left her there. In the stink and the slime from a million garbage cans, they dumped her like a load of condemned fish. There was no-one to speak over her.'

Her voice was heavy with passion now, the room vibrant with the hate that poured from the lips of the dark beauty on the couch.

'I swore to kill them. I swore many things but I did not lose control. It would be no use to fight men like that in a hot temper. I decided to have a proper plan, like a general in an army. I waited. While I waited I did what they said. I worked for Mrs. Whitton. And there I worked out what I had to do. You see, señor, I am not really a brave woman. It was no part of my plan that I should kill anyone and risk losing my own life. Other people would take the risks, and never even know why.'

'I see. Are you telling me that the others come into this as well? I mean Hudson and Hartley?'

'Yes. The four men I wanted are the four who are now dead.'

I moved around to get more comfortable in the chair.

'But chance had to come into it, surely? I mean if I hadn't started poking around how would you — '

I gradually stopped talking as the implication hit me. Isabella smiled at me lazily. There was a telephone beside the

302

television. I dialled Pop Kline's number.

'Pop? This is Preston. Did Charlie Surprise pick up that friend of ours as arranged?'

'Nope,' he replied. 'Darnedest thing. 'Bout an hour ago there's a 'phone call for the old guy. Thought you told me nobody but us knew he was here?'

'So I did, but never mind that now. What happened?'

'Well it was a woman called. After he talked to her he told me he had to leave right away. I tried to get him to wait for your friend, but he said no, it was O.K. now and he'd be on his way. He left right after. Say, Preston.'

'Yeah?'

'That man Charlie was pretty mad when he found he hadn't got a passenger. Said you promised him fifty dollars and — '

'O.K., Pop, don't worry about it. I'll see he gets it. G'bye.'

I put the 'phone down and turned to Isabella.

'So the old man was a phoney.'

'Not quite. He really is Mexican,' she

replied. 'He just isn't Juanita's father that's all. Her father died a long time ago.'

'So you hired this character to get me mixed up in this. What made you think I'd jump?'

She smiled.

'Because I have heard of you. In some ways you are a soft-hearted man. It was my judgment that you would not refuse to help an old man who walked all that way.'

I grinned wryly.

'Well, well. Good old soft-hearted sucker Preston. Just like a lamb.'

She frowned.

'Do not feel badly about it, señor. A man without compassion is less than a man.'

I grunted and sat back in my chair.

'So how much of the yarn was true? I mean the one Morales pitched me?'

'All of it. I wanted you to have correct information. Without it you could achieve nothing.'

I pulled at my ear.

'Don't try to tell me I achieved anything at all,' I protested. 'You had the whole thing mapped out. What was left?'

'Your part was very necessary, señor. There had to be someone asking questions, somebody who would not easily be discouraged.'

'So I got the part,' I muttered.

'Si. I thought it would not take you long to get as far as Hartley. And I was right, you see.'

'Let's have the rest of it.'

'Hudson was the weak one. He could not stand pain. I worked on him for a long time. Days, weeks. Always the same thing. I told him I had heard Swenson say he was a danger to them, that he knew too much. I made poor Gregg very frightened. He was expecting violence at any time.'

I said,

'When I went to his room yesterday he certainly seemed to be expecting trouble from somebody.'

'You see?' she asked. 'After you left he thought this was the time for him to get out. I had been trying to persuade him before. I promised to go with him. So now he finally made up his mind. He sent a message to Hartley for the money.'

'Why didn't he go himself?'

'Nobody ever went to Hartley's office except Mike, the man who owns the bar. If it was necessary to get in touch with Hartley, Mike took the message. When he got back from the bar, Gregg called me and told me to pack my things. Instead I telephoned Hartley and told him Gregg was going to sell you the whole story about Juanita before he left town. The fact that I took the risk of telephoning his office alone made a deep impression on Hartley. Then you arrived yourself and he was scared. It was the first time any questions from anybody had ever reached that far. Hartley tried to get in touch with Swenson, but he was out of town for the day.'

'Which you already knew, and which was part of the reason you chose yesterday,' I supplied.

'Correct. So Hartley had to do something by himself and do it right away. He knew what Swenson would have done in the same position. So he took his gun when he went to see Gregg.'

'Tell me, how could you be certain it wouldn't work out wrong?' I interjected. 'I mean what made you so sure Hudson wouldn't kill Hartley instead?'

'Why, señor, you misunderstand. It did not matter to me at all. I merely hoped one would be killed by the other. Which, was of no consequence. They fought over this ice-pick and it stuck in Gregg Hudson. Gregg must have gone for Hartley before he could draw the gun. It did not matter who died.'

And of course from her angle she had a point.

'As it happened I was lucky over Hartley. When he told Swenson what he'd done as soon as Harry got back to town, Swenson lost his temper and quarrelled with him. Swenson had been drinking a lot that night. After Hartley had gone home he kept saying he wished him dead, and cursing him. That man Bice thought it was his big opportunity to be of service. So he went to Hartley's office this morning, before the girls started work, and killed him. You were partly to blame for that.'

'Huh?' I protested. 'I don't see how I —'

'Wait, señor. Bice was present when Swenson and Hartley had their row. That was in the middle of the evening. Bice had some errands to run for Swenson, so he was out when Swenson came back from seeing you. You remember that he came to get my report after our touching little interview last night?'

'I remember,' I agreed sourly.

'Well after that Swenson was in a much better temper. Only Bice wasn't there to see that. The next thing he knew was when he was called from his bed suddenly and sent across to Mike's Bar to beat up some nosy man who was asking about Gregg Hudson. He missed the man — I think that man was you, señor — so he telephoned to Harry Swenson. All he got was abuse, so it seemed to him his boss was still in the same frame of mind. And that frame of mind meant that Hartley had to be killed.'

'I saw Swenson and Hartley last night,' I told her. 'They had a woman with them, Mrs. Whitton Junior. How about that?'

'Swenson was always very careful. He knows many people. So he had a man he knows who also knows Mrs. Whitton to ask her for a social drink. He wanted to find out exactly what she had told you.'

'And did he find out?' I questioned.

'Ah, of course. Mrs. Whitton is not famous for her discretion when she has been drinking. And Harry Swenson made certain she was drinking plenty.'

'I see.'

'He'd already talked with me about our little scene at the Hotel Miami. After that, and what he learned from Mrs. Whitton, he began to feel safe again.'

'Until Bice Smirnoff gummed up the works,' I muttered.

'As you say, señor.'

She lay there looking serenely content and yet I could sense the haunting sadness that lay behind. There didn't seem to be any point in hanging around. I got up.

'There ought to be some way to get you behind bars,' I told her.

She smiled, and swung her legs to the floor. Then she stood up too.

'If you think of one, señor, I shall be interested to hear it.'

'You're a strange, wild woman, Isabella Martinez.'

She held her head erect.

'Morales,' she corrected. 'Juanita was my baby sister.'

And that was one for the book. I looked around at the half-filled glass which remained untouched. She saw the comprehension dawning in my eyes.

'Of course,' she whispered softly. 'We always lay a place for a dead loved one.'

15

It was close to midnight when I got back to Parkside. I'd spent an hour or more drinking whisky in various bars and trying to forget the dark beauty with the branded soul.

The drinks tasted like so much soapy water and I was relieved to get into the apartment at last. I slung my jacket over a chair and loosened my tie. The buzzer sounded. Puzzled, I went to the door and opened it. A tall slim redhead smiled at me.

'May I come in?'

'Of course, er — of course,' I stammered, moving to one side.

Miss Cherry, private secretary to the indomitable Mrs Whitton Senior, slipped past me into the room. She wore a black dinner gown which was suspended precariously over her small firm breasts. It had no sides, no back, no much of anything at all above the waist. Her skin was a smooth olive colour and you could tell just by looking it would be like satin to the touch. She stood in the centre of the room looking round.

'Very nice,' she announced. 'Really very nice. I had a feeling it would be.'

I realised I was still standing at the open door. Now I shut it quickly, and walked over to her.

'When I left this afternoon, I didn't think I'd be seeing you again quite so soon, Miss Cherry.'

'It's Monica,' she said. 'You're Mark aren't you?'

I nodded. She dropped her head to one side, the deep tawny waves bunching behind. Looking at me quizzically she said,

'Is it too soon?'

'You know it isn't,' I said evenly.

'Big rugged private eye exposes himself to the timid gaze of poor country mouse private secretary.' For some reason she was mocking me. 'Well we're not in the country now. That makes me a town mouse, wouldn't you say?'

'Beautiful, I would say anything you

312

wanted, right this minute.'

I meant it.

'Remember what you said this afternoon?'

'I think so.' I pretended to concentrate. 'I said we could have a few drinks and see what develops.'

'Right.'

She stepped the yard that separated us. There were lights dancing in the hazel eyes.

'Would you mind if we had the drinks some other time?'

'It's late for drinking anyway,' I whispered.

She slipped a smooth arm round my neck.

'So why don't we just see what develops?'

And I have a golden rule.

Never argue with a dame.

YOU'RE BETTER OFF DEAD
NO GOLD WHEN YOU GO
MURDER IS FOR KEEPS
THIS'LL KILL YOU
NOBODY LIVES FOREVER
NOTHING PERSONAL
DON'T BOTHER TO KNOCK

We do hope that you have enjoyed reading this large print book.

Did you know that all of our titles are available for purchase?

We publish a wide range of high quality large print books including:
Romances, Mysteries, Classics
General Fiction
Non Fiction and Westerns

Special interest titles available in large print are:
The Little Oxford Dictionary
Music Book, Song Book
Hymn Book, Service Book

Also available from us courtesy of Oxford University Press:
Young Readers' Dictionary
(large print edition)
Young Readers' Thesaurus
(large print edition)

For further information or a free brochure, please contact us at:
Ulverscroft Large Print Books Ltd.,
The Green, Bradgate Road, Anstey,
Leicester, LE7 7FU, England.
Tel: (00 44) **0116 236 4325**
Fax: (00 44) **0116 234 0205**

Other titles in the
Linford Mystery Library:

DEATH OF A
LOW HANDICAP MAN

Brian Ball

When Tom Tyzack is viciously beaten to death with a golf club on the local golf course, PC Arthur Root, the local village bobby, is in the unenviable position of having to question his fellow club members. He is regarded with scorn by the detective in charge of the case, and the latter's ill-natured attitude toward the suspects does little to assist him in solving the mystery. But it is Root who, after a second brutal murder, stumbles on the clue that leads to the discovery of the murderer's identity.

ONE SWORD LESS

Colin D. Peel

Working on a defence project in a Research Laboratory, electronic engineer Richard Brendon discovers that he has become part of the cold war. Agonisingly, Brendon is required to balance the lives of his wife and children against co-operation with a foreign power. Forced to use his technical expertise to further a plan to precipitate nuclear war, he takes desperate action to prevent the project and save millions of people from certain destruction.

POSTMAN'S KNOCK

J. F. Straker

Inspector Pitt has a problem. The postman in Grange Road has mysteriously vanished. Had he absconded with the mail — been kidnapped or perhaps murdered? And why had he delivered only some of the letters? The people of Grange Road seem averse to police inquiries. Was there a conspiracy to remove the postman? Before any questions are answered assault, blackmail and sudden death disturb the normal peace of Grange Road.

ONE TO JUMP

George Douglas

When Detective Sergeant Dick Garrett spends his leave in Wellesbourne Green to persuade ex-crook Molly Bilton to marry him, he is faced with a mystery. Ace criminal Flint, previously known to Molly, is found dead with no clues to the killer. An assault on Gypsy Ben Thompson's daughter leads Garrett to risk his future in the Force. He suspects that one of the local police could be involved working hand in glove with the dead man.

REFLECTED GLORY

John Russell Fearn

When artist Clive Hexley, R.A. vanishes, Chief Inspector Calthorp of Scotland Yard is called upon to look into the disappearance, and his investigations lead him to question Hexley's ex-fiancée, Elsa Farraday. Elsa confesses that she has murdered the artist. The girl's peculiar manner puzzles Calthorp, and he hesitates to make an arrest, particularly as Hexley's body cannot be found. It is not until Calthorp calls in Dr. Adam Castle, the psychiatrist investigator, that the strange mystery of Elsa's behaviour and the artist's disappearance is solved.

A HEARSE FOR McNALLY

G. J. Barrett

Gerry Westmayne had worked out how to steal the State Jewels of Lahkpore. McNally carried out the plan but, with cracksman Herb Setters, he stole the loot from Westmayne's safe only to discover that it was worthless. McNally had been outsmarted, and he began to wonder if he could trust Gilda Kemp. And after killing his boss he realized the extent of his girlfriend's treachery and learned too late the high cost of a place in the sun.